A Wish Comes True

There was an expression in the Earl's eyes that Olivia did not understand.

"What I want you to tell me," the Earl said, "and you have promised to tell me the truth, is why you did not let me die?"

Because it was so strange a question, Olivia just stared at him.

Then as she sought for words with which to reply she knew the answer.

Slowly, as her heart told her she loved him, the colour spread over her cheeks like the dawn sweeping up the sky.

The truth flashed through her like forked lightning.

Then as her lips could not move and it was impossible to say a word, the Earl said very quietly:

"That is what I hoped was the reason!"

A Camfield Novel of Love
by Barbara Cartland

———

"Barbara Cartland's novels are all distinguished by their intelligence, good sense, and good nature...."
— **ROMANTIC TIMES**

"Who could give better advice on how to keep your romance going strong than the world's most famous romance novelist, Barbara Cartland?"
— **THE STAR**

Camfield Place,
Hatfield
Hertfordshire,
England

Dearest Reader,

Camfield Novels of Love mark a very exciting era of my books with Jove. They have already published nearly two hundred of my titles since they became my first publisher in America, and now all my original paperback romances in the future will be published exclusively by them.

As you already know, Camfield Place in Hertfordshire is my home, which originally existed in 1275, but was rebuilt in 1867 by the grandfather of Beatrix Potter.

It was here in this lovely house, with the best view in the county, that she wrote *The Tale of Peter Rabbit*. Mr. McGregor's garden is exactly as she described it. The door in the wall that the fat little rabbit could not squeeze underneath and the goldfish pool where the white cat sat twitching its tail are still there.

I had Camfield Place blessed when I came here in 1950 and was so happy with my husband until he died, and now with my children and grandchildren, that I know the atmosphere is filled with love and we have all been very lucky.

It is easy here to write of love and I know you will enjoy the Camfield Novels of Love. Their plots are definitely exciting and the covers very romantic. They come to you, like all my books, with love.

Bless you,

CAMFIELD NOVELS OF LOVE

by Barbara Cartland

A NEW CAMFIELD NOVEL OF LOVE BY

BARBARA CARTLAND

A Wish Comes True

J

JOVE BOOKS, NEW YORK

A WISH COMES TRUE

A Jove Book / published by arrangement with
the author

PRINTING HISTORY
Jove edition / August 1992

ISBN: 0-515-10904-5

Jove Books are published by The Berkley Publishing Group,
200 Madison Avenue, New York, New York 10016.
The name "JOVE" and the "J" logo
are trademarks belonging to Jove Publications, Inc.

PRINTED IN THE UNITED STATES OF AMERICA

10 9 8 7 6 5 4 3 2 1

Author's Note

THE Power of Attorney is usually in use when someone with money—an elderly woman or man— is too old or mentally unstable to conduct their own affairs.

Then the power of signing cheques and organising an Estate or business is given to a relation or to a solicitor who acts as an Executor.

It has very old origins—in fact the beginning of it has been lost in the midst of time.

It arose originally out of Common Law and in particular the general law of agency.

Merchants authorised a subordinate to buy goods for them in distant countries and eventually the law developed so that this became entirely legal.

Various cases came before the Courts over the years which clarified some of the ways it can be used.

There was, however, no legislation at that time and it goes so far back that the original date is not given in the legal textbooks.

The case that I have put in this novel would have been entirely legal at that date, so long as the solicitors in charge of the Estate had the Earl's signature.

Of course, there have been abuses of this arrangement, but on the whole in England it has worked very well and a great many businesses, Estates, and fortunes have been saved by the original owner giving Power of Attorney to someone younger, more knowledgeable, and, in a great number of cases, with a keenness to try new ideas and new methods.

chapter one

1824

OLIVIA looked in her purse and sighed.

She realised they were growing very short of money.

Sooner or later she would have to approach the new Earl of Chadwood.

She had hoped that he would call on her, or at least send a message inviting her to Chad.

But so far they had heard nothing from him.

She knew it would be a great mistake to push herself on him as soon as he arrived.

After all, as she was well aware, everything was new to him, and he had never expected to inherit the title.

A distant Cousin, he was soldiering in the East when he had been informed that the 5th Earl had died and his two sons had been lost at sea.

Both William and John were keen on sailing.

They had gone to the Estate in Cornwall which their father owned.

Daringly, they had put to sea when there was a storm blowing up.

They had both been drowned, and it had been a body-blow for the Earl, who was already in bad health.

It had also distressed everyone on the Estate.

They had loved William and John and had watched them growing up with the same interest and affection as they had for their own children.

Olivia found it hard to believe they were dead.

The two young men had been like brothers to her and part of her life since she was born.

After their Father died, nearly a year passed before the new Earl arrived from the East.

Nobody knew anything about him except that he was a Cousin.

They had hoped that things would go on as they always had done.

The old servants at Chad looked after the great house as if it belonged to them personally.

The farmers and workers on the Estate strove to make it the envy of every other Landlord.

For Olivia it had been a miserable year, not only because the old Earl had died, as she had always thought from a broken heart, but so had her Father.

He had been driving his Chaise, drawn by one horse, to visit a sick parishioner.

As he reached the end of the village, a large Phaeton with four horses swept round the corner.

The driver, a smart Buck from London, was drunk and reckless.

The vehicles collided, and while the Buck survived, the Vicar was killed.

The Reverend Arthur Lambrick had been the Vicar of the parish and Private Chaplain to the Earl for twenty-four years.

He was an extremely intelligent as well as a good-looking man, but he had never recovered from the shock of losing his wife.

She had died the previous year of a fever which had swept over the countryside.

People said it was the beginning of a new Plague.

Others averred that it was the punishment of God for the wickedness and immorality which was rife in London.

However, after killing a number of old people as well as the beautiful and much-loved wife of the Vicar, it faded away.

There were no more cases for the Doctors to shake their heads over.

Olivia, who was nearly nineteen, found herself with no one to turn to for help.

She had with her at home her small sister, Wendy, and her brother, Anthony, during the School holidays.

Anthony, who was always called Tony, had just finished his schooling at Eton.

The old Earl had promised to send him to Oxford, where his Father had been.

He was due to go there in October.

Olivia was praying that the new Earl would carry out the commitments of his predecessor.

The difficulty was that until he arrived, she was desperately short of money.

Until he did so, the Solicitors had refused to continue her Mother's allowance.

She had been a Wood and had always received

an allowance of two hundred pounds a year from the Head of the Family.

It was the tradition in England that all the money belonged to the man who bore the title.

He normally shared out amongst his relatives what he could afford.

This kept them living happily and comfortably in the way to which they were accustomed.

Without her Mother's allowance and with no pension for her Father, things, Olivia found, were getting desperate.

There had been a small amount of money in the Bank.

That was practically finished.

She was uncomfortably aware that almost as soon as the new owner took up residence, she would have to speak to him.

"I am sure he will understand," she told herself optimistically.

At the same time, she felt very nervous.

She counted what was in her purse.

There was very little.

Then she took out half a sovereign, which was Bessie's wages for three weeks.

She felt embarrassed at not paying her recently.

But she had to keep some money for the food they ate, and Tony had a large appetite.

They lived on the rabbits which the village boys snared in the woods.

These had been neglected after the old Earl's death.

Otherwise, Olivia knew, they would often have been very hungry.

Now she supposed the Game-keepers would no

longer "turn a blind eye" to what was happening.

She could not afford even the cheapest cuts of meat from the Butcher's.

There were a large number of people in the village in the same plight.

The new Earl's Solicitor had been very firm that he had no authority to pay out money without instructions.

In her Father's absence it was Olivia who pleaded with him almost on her knees.

How could he, she asked, not continue to provide the old people with the small pension they had received every week?

"If you do not do so." she said, "they will die, and that will be on your conscience for the rest of your life!"

"You are asking me to do something which is illegal, Miss Lambrick," the elderly Solicitor replied.

"Illegal or not, it is merciful," Olivia said, "and, as you are aware, it is a miracle that with so little food some of the older people survived the winter."

She had finally persuaded him to give them half their pensions, and somehow they had managed.

She thought, however, that the whole village looked thin and pale.

She could only pray every night that the Earl would be home soon.

He would then understand that something needed to be done immediately.

"I expect Papa would have talked to him by this time," she told herself, "but it is very difficult for me. I do not want him to think I am interfering."

Actually, she knew she was already rather frightened by what she had heard about the Earl.

He had at last come home.

Of course, nothing else had been discussed in the village since his arrival.

She learnt from Bessie when she came in to clean the house and cook that the old servants thought him a very strange man indeed.

" 'There's no warmth in 'im,' Mr. Upton says," Bessie related.

Upton, the Butler, had been at Chad for nearly forty years.

Olivia knew he was a good judge of character.

Then she learnt that the new Earl was looking through the account books.

These had been kept very neatly for years by the Secretary to the Estate, Mr. Bentick.

It seemed strange that he should be first concerning himself with expenditure.

He should be meeting his tenants, farmers, and employees, who were all longing to see him.

Olivia told herself she must not criticise.

It would be a mistake and something her Father would deplore.

She shut her purse and put it in her hand-bag, then laid the bag by the desk in the Sitting-Room, wondering what she could do.

Should she go up to the "Big House" this afternoon and introduce herself?

"It is too soon!" she said aloud.

Even as she spoke she heard a heavy knock on the front-door.

She went from the pretty Sitting-Room into the hall.

Standing outside was one of the older boys from the village who sometimes ran messages for her.

He was red in the face and breathless, as if he had been running.

"What is it, Ted?" she asked.

"It be terrible noos, Miss Olivia—terrible!" Ted gasped.

"About what?" Olivia asked nervously.

"Mister Tony."

Olivia gave a little cry.

"What has happened? He is not . . . hurt?"

" 'E's bin arrested, Miss Olivia! Arrested by two of th' new grooms up at t'Big 'Ouse! They're accusin' 'im o' stealin'!"

"Stealing!" Olivia exclaimed. "What can you mean?"

"Mister Tony went ridin' orf wi' one o' t' 'orses as belongs to 'Is Lordship. A big black stallion, it were. 'E takes it over t'jumps, ridin' like wot 'e always do!"

Ted paused for breath, and Olivia said:

"Go on!"

"They goes after 'e and taks 'e straight up t'the 'ouse an' shuts 'e in t'stables an' goes an tell 'Is Lordship as 'e's a thief!"

"I have never heard anything so ridiculous!" Olivia said.

She was relieved that Tony was not hurt.

But it was very unfortunate that the new grooms had not understood that Tony had always been allowed by the previous Earl to exercise the horses.

He would also have thought it a great joke if one was left unattended to jump on its back and ride off on it.

"What was the horse doing with no one holding it?" she asked.

"Oi see there be three grooms exercisin' t' 'orses," Ted explained, "an' they 'ears a rabbit screaming in a trap in th' wood."

Olivia guessed it was one of Ted's traps, but she did not say so and he went on:

"One o' t'grooms goes an' set it free an' th' other two goes into th' wood with 'im."

He grinned as he finished:

"Mister Tony sees th' big stallion tied t' a post, jumps on 'e, an' rides away!"

Olivia could see it happening.

Tony had been very restless this last week since the Earl was in residence.

She had told him he could not ride the horses as he always had.

"We must wait for the new Earl's permission to borrow his horses from the stables," she said firmly.

"How is he to know that is what I do if I do not meet him?" Tony asked subtly.

"You will meet him sooner or later," Olivia replied, "and you know it would be a mistake to ask for favours the very moment he arrives."

Tony, instead of riding, had therefore walked in the woods or sat about the house, grumbling.

"Farmer Johnson thinks it extremely remiss of His Lordship not to have called on him yet," he had announced. "And Lady Marriott sent him an invitation to have tea with her to which he never replied."

Lady Marriott was very old and almost blind.

Olivia could not help feeling slightly sympathetic at the Earl's delay in answering her invitation.

At the same time, it was quite unnecessary to be rude.

"The Woods have always had the most beautiful manners," her Mother said when they were children, "and I would not wish you to be the exception to the rule."

They had therefore been brought up to think of other people rather than themselves.

They were charming to everybody, as their Mother and Father were, from the highest to the lowest.

Olivia now said:

"Thank you, Ted, for coming and telling me at once! I will go up to the Big House and explain to His Lordship that Mister Tony was not really stealing the horse."

"Oi 'opes as 'e'll listen to ye, Miss 'livia," Ted said. "Them as 'ave met 'Is Lordship says as 'e gives 'em th' cold shivers!"

Olivia was not listening.

She was hurrying upstairs to fetch her bonnet.

Having told Bessie where she was going, she set off the quickest way through the Park to Chad House.

In fact, Green Gables, the house in which they lived, was on the very edge of the Park.

She did not, therefore, have to go out into the road or even through the gates to reach her destination.

Instead, she walked under the great oak trees.

She moved so lightly that she hardly disturbed the spotted deer who were lying in their shade.

At any other time she would have appreciated

the beauty of the lake which reflected the blue of the sky.

The house itself, with its hundreds of windows and the ancient statues on the roof, was silhouetted against the sky.

She loved Chad because she had been allowed to go there ever since she was a small child.

She thought she knew every inch of it, and that it was a part of her.

She was hurrying, knowing that Tony, if he was really locked up in the stables, would be fretting.

He would resent being imprisoned and the discomfort of it.

She was thankful as she reached the front-door to see that it was opened by Upton, the Butler.

"Good-morning, Miss Olivia!" he said in his deep, well-modulated voice.

"Good-morning, Upton! I hear Mr. Tony is in trouble! Can I see His Lordship?"

She thought Upton hesitated before he said:

"If you'll wait in the Morning-Room, Miss Olivia, I'll ask His Lordship if he can see you."

He looked so worried as he left that Olivia wondered if the Earl was seriously annoyed with Tony.

Then she told herself he could not be so foolish as not to realise it was just a boyish prank.

* * *

When Upton left Olivia he went from the large hall with its beautifully carved statues and gilt-framed portraits to the Study.

He reached the door, then hesitated when he heard raised voices.

Inside the Study, Gerald Wood was saying:

"If you do not help me, then I shall doubtless be taken to prison, and that will cause a scandal in the family!"

"You can hardly blame me for that!" the Earl replied.

He spoke in a cold, rather clipped voice.

Sitting at the desk, he was an exceedingly handsome man.

But his grey eyes were hard and his lips when he shut them were set in a tight line.

Anyone looking at him would have known from the way he carried himself that he was a soldier.

When he moved and spoke, it was as if he were still on parade.

"Now, listen," Gerald Wood said, "I know I have been extravagant, and I admit I have made a fool of myself, but Cousin Edward always helped me out."

There was silence. Then he added:

"After all, I *am* your half-brother!"

"*Half* being the operative word!" the Earl remarked dryly.

Gerald stared at him.

He had never thought there was any likelihood of anyone other than William or John, with whom he had been close friends, inheriting the title.

Yet in their place there was this strange, harsh man.

He was a man, Gerald felt, with whom he had nothing in common.

It was, he supposed, understandable when he remembered the history of the new Earl.

He had heard it repeated and repeated since he was a child.

His Father had married first, when he was quite a young man, a woman called Hannah.

She came from a well-known family, and it was considered an excellent marriage for both the young people concerned.

However, no one had taken into account that their temperaments were entirely different.

Lionel Wood was a "Happy-go-lucky," charming man who made friends wherever he went.

He was adored by those who served him.

"Give him another chance!" he would say if anyone did anything wrong.

Gerald had thought his Father the most marvellous man in the world.

He had learnt, however, as soon as he was old enough to understand, how unhappy he had been.

His Father's first wife, Hannah, had been a strait-laced, censorious woman who suspected the worst of everyone.

She disliked her husband's friends.

She had been extremely shocked by the *Beau Ton* of London in which they moved.

She continually found fault with her husband, and with everybody else in the houses in which they lived.

Finally, when the tension between them grew unbearable, she had left.

She returned to her parents, taking with her, without Lionel Wood's consent, their only child, a son who was christened Lenox.

It took five years for Lionel Wood to divorce her for desertion.

When he had done so, he married again.

His new wife was very much like himself.

She was always laughing, full of the joy of life, and extremely kind to those around her.

When Gerald was born she knew she had made up to her husband for the son he had lost.

Lionel Wood had been too proud to ask Hannah to return Lenox to him.

Anyway, he was heir to very little.

It had not been particularly important that he should have a son to follow him.

Gerald could never remember when his home was not filled with happiness and laughter.

If they had to live carefully because there was not much money, no one worried about it.

It was, however, understandable that when he reached manhood he wanted to enjoy himself in London.

When first his Father, then his Mother, was no longer there, he threw caution to the winds.

He spent his time with the Bucks and *Beaux* of St. James's and indulged in the extravagances initiated by George IV.

Gerald, or "Gerry," as they all called him, was thrilled with everything, from the mills that took place on Wimbledon Common to the racing at Newmarket.

He enjoyed gambling at Crockford's and Wattier's and inevitably the pretty "Cyprians."

They abounded at "The White House" and dozens of other Houses of Pleasure.

His Cousin, the 5th Earl, had paid his debts half a dozen times.

It was only a week ago, when the Duns were actually hammering on the door, that he realised once again he had gone too far.

He knew then that he would have to seek the assistance of the new Head of the Family.

The 6th Earl was, in fact, his half-brother, Lenox.

He posted down to Chad, thinking be must certainly ingratiate himself with the relation he had never met.

Lenox Wood had actually been forgotten by all his relations until they realised his new-found importance to them personally.

"You cannot be serious!" Gerry said now in his most beguiling voice. "Cousin Edward always understood and said 'Boys will be boys!' "

"I should have thought," the Earl said in a chilling tone, "that you would consider yourself a man by this time, and try to behave like one!"

"I promise you I will 'turn over a new leaf,' " Gerry said. "If you will pay my debts and give me the same allowance which Cousin Edward did, I will stick to the 'straight and narrow.' Is that a deal?"

"If you mean by that," the Earl said slowly, "what you have just said, the answer is 'No!' "

Gerry stared at him.

"Do you mean you are not going to help me or give me an allowance?"

"Why should I?" the Earl asked. "I have earned my own keep all these years. I see no reason why I should pander to parasites or pay for their riotous living!"

"But that is exactly what the Head of the Family has to do!" Gerry argued.

"Then where the Woods are concerned they are going to be disappointed," the Earl said. "I have no intention, and let me say this again, of paying

14

large allowances to young men who do not work! Nor will I wrap up in cotton-wool a lot of decrepit old people who should have saved during their lifetimes."

Because he could hardly believe what he was hearing, Gerry sat down in a chair facing the desk.

"Now, let us talk about this sensibly," he said. "I know I should not have bothered you so soon, but I am hard pressed, and I felt sure you would be sympathetic."

The Earl looked at him as if he were inspecting some strange insect.

"You have your health and strength," he said. "I imagine you can find employment of some sort, and for your own sake, it should be as soon as possible!"

"Good God, what do you think I can do?" Gerry exclaimed. "And anyway, what I could earn would be only a 'drop in the ocean' as regards my debts!"

"Then I can only say," the Earl replied dryly, "that you will doubtless find it somewhat uncomfortable in the Fleet!"

As this was the name of the Debtors' Prison, Gerry knew he was taunting him.

Instinctively he clenched his hands.

Then he knew it would be a mistake to hit his brother, which was what he longed to do.

Instead, he said:

"I suppose you will give me a bed for the night? Then we can talk about this later. I feel sure when you think it over you will realise where your duty lies."

The Earl gave a short laugh which had no humour in it.

"I have no wish to raise your hopes," he said, "but I will of course, as you have come so far, put you up for the night."

"That is very kind of you."' Gerry said.

He could not prevent the hint of sarcasm in his voice.

Then, as if he knew it would be a mistake to say any more, he walked out of the Study.

He nearly collided with Upton, who was standing outside.

He walked past him without a word.

Upton, who had known him ever since he was in his perambulator, looked after him.

The worried expression on his face increased.

He then went into the Study.

"Excuse me, M'Lord," he said, "but Miss Olivia Lambrick's here to see Your Lordship."

The Earl did not answer, and Upton went on:

"It'll be about her brother, Master Anthony, who's being held by th' grooms in the stables."

"Who is Miss Lambrick?" the Earl asked stiffly.

"Miss Olivia Lambrick, M'Lord, is the daughter of th' late Reverend Arthur Lambrick, who was th' Vicar here for twenty-four years, and was also His Lordship's Private Chaplain."

The Earl made a note on a piece of paper which lay on the desk in front of him.

Upton went on:

"He were a fine man, M'Lord, and a great loss to th' village. His wife were one of th' family before she wed and was loved by everybody. There wasn't a dry eye in th' Churchyard when she were buried!"

The Earl made another note before he said:

"Show Miss Lambrick in."

"Very good, M'Lord."

Upton went back down the passage and into the Morning-Room, where Olivia was waiting.

She turned round eagerly as he came through the door.

"His Lordship will see me?" she asked before Upton could speak.

"Yes, Miss Olivia," he said, "but . . ."

He waited until she came to his side, then said in a low voice:

"His Lordship's been a bit upset by Master Gerry."

"Is Gerry here?" Olivia asked. "How lovely! I have not seen him for a long time!"

Upton did not say any more.

Olivia, however, was aware that the elderly man was perturbed as he walked ahead of her, and wondered why.

He opened the Study door.

"Miss Olivia Lambrick, M'Lord!" he announced.

Olivia went in.

She was looking very lovely with her small oval face and huge eyes framed by her chip-straw bonnet.

It was decorated with cornflowers and blue ribbons.

Her face was pale and she was very thin.

Her gown was old, but it did not disguise the soft curves of her breasts, her tiny waist, or the grace with which she moved.

She walked to the desk and held out her hand.

"Welcome to Chad, My Lord!" she said. "I am so delighted to meet you, and have looked forward eagerly to your return."

The Earl had risen slowly to his feet.

His hand took hers and she felt his fingers were cold.

"Will you sit down, Miss Lambrick," he said. "I understand you are another relation."

He did not make it sound as if it pleased him, but Olivia replied:

"Yes, Mama was the late Earl's first Cousin, so I suppose she would be your third or fourth."

She gave a little light laugh which was very musical.

Then, as the Earl did not speak, she said in a more serious tone:

"I have come to see you about my brother, Anthony, or Tony, as we always call him. I am afraid he has been rather mischievous and has upset your grooms!"

"I hardly think stealing a stallion can be described as mischievous!" the Earl said stiffly.

Olivia laughed.

"Of course he was not stealing it!" she replied. "He has always been allowed to ride any horse he wishes from the Chad stables."

"He has not had my permission to do so!" the Earl said.

"I know, and it was very naughty of him," Olivia replied. "I have told him over and over again he must not impose on you until you find your bearings, but the temptation was too great."

She saw that the Earl did not understand, and explained:

"The groom who was riding the stallion was attending to a trapped rabbit in the woods. The horse was left unattended, and Tony, who happened to be walking by, jumped onto its back and rode off, taking all the high jumps as he did so."

She paused, and after what seemed to her a long silence, the Earl said:

"Is that the sort of behaviour I can expect from my relatives?"

"Tony will make his apologies," Olivia said, "and please accept mine. But it has been a very boring time for him, waiting to see you to ask if he can go on helping to exercise the horses as he has always done in the past."

"I have grooms to do that!" the Earl said coldly.

Olivia looked at him in consternation.

"Do you mean you will not allow us in future to borrow horses from the stables?"

"Shall I say I will consider it!" the Earl said slowly.

Olivia was about to plead with him when she remembered she had more important things to discuss.

A little nervously she said:

"Now that I am here, I wonder if I might talk to you about our future?"

"Your—future?" the Earl said in an uncompromising tone.

"You see . . . Mama always received an allowance of two hundred pounds a year from Cousin Edward. But when he died, the Solicitors said they had no authority to continue to pay it."

The Earl did not speak, and Olivia went on quickly:

"Papa had been the Vicar and Chaplain for twenty-four years, and of course he had expected to receive a pension which would continue after his death."

The Earl's face was expressionless, but Olivia felt he was unsympathetic, and she continued nervously:

"I was waiting for an opportunity to speak to you, but we are practically penniless, and it is something which cannot continue for very much longer!"

"And you really think, Miss Lambrick, that I should provide you with an allowance that ceased with your parents' death?"

"If you ... do not do so," Olivia said, "we ... shall all ... three ... starve!"

She tried to speak lightly.

But because she was frightened, there was a sob in her voice.

"Who owns the house in which you are living?" the Earl asked.

"That is ... another thing I wanted to ... speak to you about," Olivia said. "Papa was given Green Gables when he married Mama for the simple reason that the Vicarage, which is next to the Church, was, and still is, in a very dilapidated state. There never seemed any reason to restore it."

She paused and then went on:

"But now ... if you appoint another Vicar, which I suppose you must do, I have ... no idea ... where we ... shall go."

"And again you think that is my business!" the Earl said.

Olivia hesitated.

"There is ... no one else who can ... help me ... and I was ... certain that was ... what you would ... want to ... do."

"I do not follow your reasoning," the Earl remarked. "I do not know you or your brother and sister. Your Father is of no further use to me, and your Mother, who you say was a relation, is dead!"

"But . . . we—their children—are alive!" Olivia said.

The Earl looked at her in what she thought was a hostile fashion.

"I imagine, Miss Lambrick," he said slowly, "that you have some talents which will enable you to earn enough money to keep you. And your brother, if he rides as well as you say, could be employed looking after horses. If you cannot support your younger sister, there are, I believe, Orphanages for the children of the Clergy."

Olivia just stared at him.

She could not believe what she was hearing.

She went very pale and thought for a moment she must faint.

Then she told herself she had to fight not for herself, but for Tony and Wendy.

As she thought it, she suddenly remembered the pensioners!

In a voice that did not sound like her own, she said:

"The pensioners have been . . . waiting anxiously in the village for . . . you to arrive . . . because it was only with the . . . greatest difficulty that I . . . persuaded the . . . Solicitors to . . . give them a little . . . money to save them from dying during the . . . Winter without . . . heat and without . . . food."

Olivia drew a deep breath and went on:

21

"I know my Father . . . if he had been alive . . . would have . . . reassured them that . . . you would be . . . generous where they are . . . concerned."

"As your Father is dead," the Earl said, "I think, Miss Lambrick, that is hardly your business!"

"On the contrary, it is the business of every decent Christian person who has watched . . . because you have been so long in coming home . . . the old people growing . . . more and more . . . fragile . . . week by week . . . month by month."

"The reason why I was delayed coming back from India," the Earl said, "is that the voyage round the Cape inevitably takes a long time."

"It was a . . . long time for . . . those who were hungry . . . and for . . . those who have . . . no work . . . because there was . . . no one to . . . employ them."

The Earl's lips tightened.

"That, again, is my business, Miss Lambrick."

"I agree," Olivia said, "they are . . . your people. They have been part of Chad ever since they . . . were born. They have been . . . loyal to this . . . house and to . . . the Earl who lives . . . in it. They will be . . . loyal to you . . . if you . . . care for them and . . . look after them as your . . . predecessor did!"

"I expected when I came home to hear the eternal cry of 'This is how it is always done,' and that every change would be violently resisted!"

"What I am talking about is not change, My Lord, but . . . survival!" Olivia said slowly.

For a moment the Earl just stared across the desk at her.

Then he rose to his feet.

"I think it would be a mistake to continue this conversation," he said coldly.

Olivia rose too.

"I have to know," she said in a small voice, "exactly where I stand . . . are you seriously telling . . . me that you will not . . . give us any . . . money at all . . . and that we are to . . . move out of Green Gables as soon as you have . . . appointed another . . . incumbent?"

"You have put it very concisely, Miss Lambrick!" the Earl said.

He held out his hand.

"And now, as I am very busy, I hope you will understand—there is nothing more to be said."

Feeling as if she were so dazed that she could not think clearly, Olivia found it impossible to move.

She just stood staring at him.

Her eyes seemed to fill her face, and there was a stricken look in them which it was impossible for the Earl not to notice.

He looked at her.

Then he said in a different tone:

"I have an idea which perhaps might work!"

He sat down again and rang the gold bell which stood on the desk.

The door opened almost immediately.

Olivia knew that Upton had been outside, doubtless listening to what was being said.

"Fetch Mr. Gerald!" the Earl commanded.

"Very good, M'Lord."

The Earl was writing something on a piece of paper, and Olivia did not speak or move.

She felt as if somebody had dealt her a blow on the head and she was almost unconscious.

What could she do? How could she let Tony and Wendy starve?

How could she face the village, knowing they would expect her to intercede on their behalf?

It seemed as if a century passed before the door opened and Gerald came in.

There was something alert and vital about him, as if he thought his half-brother had changed his mind.

Then, when he saw Olivia, he smiled.

"Hello, Olivia!" he said. "I did not know you were here!"

He saw how pale she was, and he looked suspiciously at the Earl.

"What has happened?" he asked. "You have not been unkind to Olivia? I can tell you she is a very special person, and Cousin Edward thought there was no one like her."

"Miss Lambrick," the Earl said in his hard voice, "had been beseeching me in the same way you have been in much the same trouble."

"Debts!" Gerald said with a wry twist to his lips.

"No . . . not debts." Olivia said before the Earl could speak. "It is . . . just that we have . . . no money left . . . and His Lordship . . . will not continue Mama's . . . allowance or . . . give us any . . . of Papa's pension . . . now that he is . . . dead!"

Her voice broke on the last word and her eyes filled with tears.

"Good God!" Gerald exclaimed. "You are not going to cheese-pare Olivia and everyone in the village and, I suppose, the entire Estate into penury?"

He looked aggressively at his half-brother as he spoke.

The Earl, sitting upright in his chair, merely replied:

"As I have already said to Miss Lambrick—that is my business!"

"That is not true," Gerald contradicted. "You are the Head of the Family, and you hold the house, the Estate, the villagers, and everything else only in trust to you for your lifetime. You cannot dispose of it because it is entailed, and you cannot take it with you when you die! It is up to you to look after those who are dependent on you."

He spoke violently, but the Earl remained unmoved.

Then he said:

"I sent for you, Gerald, because I have a proposition to put to you regarding Miss Lambrick."

"A—proposition?" Gerald enquired.

"I have listened to two tales of woe," the Earl went on, and there was a sarcastic note in his voice, "and I have heard from you both that you expect me to assume responsibility for your plight simply because the Wood blood runs in all our veins."

"That is right," Gerald said sharply.

"Then if you force me to do something for you, which is against all my inclinations, I have a solution to your problem and to Miss Lambrick's."

"And what is that?" Gerald asked warily.

"You, Gerald," the Earl said, "have got yourself into a disastrous predicament entirely through your own fault and your own lack of intelligence."

Gerald drew in his breath, but he did not speak, and the Earl went on:

"What you must do in the future is to lead a sensible life, and perhaps you should have a wife. That might prevent you, if nothing else, from running after 'Cyprians' and throwing your money away on the green-baize tables."

"A—wife?" Gerald exclaimed.

"That is what I said," the Earl replied, "and it seems to me appropriate that you should marry your Cousin. She has no one to look after her and, as I need the house in which she is living, nowhere to go!"

Because she had not had the slightest idea of what he was going to say, Olivia could only gasp.

Then she knew she must be dreaming.

No man could have suggested anything so utterly and completely impossible.

chapter two

THERE was what seemed to be a long silence. Then Gerald said:

"Do you know what you are saying?"

"Of course I do," the Earl replied, "and it is sheer common sense!"

"I think it is the most absurd, the most outrageous suggestion I have ever heard!" Gerald said slowly.

The Earl shrugged his shoulders.

"Very well," he said, "You have the choice. You can each of you go your own way, but let me make it clear I will not raise a finger to help either of you."

He walked towards the door.

Then Olivia said in a voice that did not sound like her own:

"Can we . . . please have . . . time to . . . think about it?"

For a moment the Earl hesitated, and she thought he was going to refuse.

Then he said:

"You can give me your decision this evening, and I refuse to listen to any more arguments!"

He left the Study as he spoke, shutting the door sharply behind him.

Olivia looked at Gerald.

"It . . . cannot be . . . true!" she whispered.

Gerald did not answer.

He walked across the room to stand at the open window as if he needed fresh air to help him breathe.

"What . . . can we . . . do?" Olivia asked when he did not speak. "If we . . . refuse, he will . . . turn us into the street . . . and we will . . . starve . . . with the . . . pensioners."

"The—pensioners?" Gerald asked.

"They are only just . . . surviving on the . . . pittance the Solicitors gave them . . . until he should . . . return. I am . . . sure he . . . intends to leave them as . . . they are . . . and most of . . . them are . . . hungry!"

Gerald stiffened. Then he said:

"My debts are nearly ten thousand pounds. If I do not settle them, I will be sent to prison."

Olivia gave a cry.

"Not . . . prison . . . Gerry?"

"Yes. The Fleet," he answered, "and, quite frankly, I would rather die!"

Olivia got to her feet.

"I must go . . . home," she said. "I cannot think . . . clearly here. I suppose . . . although I did not ask him, I can take . . . Tony with . . . me."

"What is wrong with Tony?" Gerald enquired.

"He rode one of the Earl's . . . horses and the grooms whom he . . . brought down from . . . London thought he was . . . stealing it. So he is . . . locked up in the . . . stables."

Gerald turned from the window and put his hand up to his forehead.

"This becomes more and more absurd, like a novelette which in real life nobody would believe was true."

"But . . . it is . . . true!" Olivia said faintly. "And I . . . want to . . . go home and . . . think."

She walked a little unsteadily towards the door.

"I am coming with you!" Gerald said. "I cannot stay in this house and not strike my half-brother, which is what he deserves."

Olivia opened the door.

"Come with me . . . if you . . . like," she said, "but I warn you . . . there is . . . little or . . . nothing . . . to eat!"

Gerald's lips tightened. Then he said:

"We will soon remedy that if Mrs. Banks is still here."

"Of course . . . she is . . . here," Olivia answered. "I could not . . . imagine Chad . . . without Mrs. Banks."

"Nor could I," Gerald agreed.

He took Olivia by the arm, and they walked down the passage until they reached the hall.

There was no sign of Upton.

They moved on towards the kitchen-quarters, which were beyond the Dining-Room.

Just before they reached them, a door opened and Mr. Bentick came out of the Estate Office.

"Oh, there you are, Miss Olivia!" he said. "I heard

you were in the house, and I wanted to see you."

He spoke in an urgent manner which made Olivia aware that something was wrong.

"I . . . I was just . . . going home . . . Mr. Bentick," she said.

"Will you come into the office for a moment?" he begged.

"Y-yes . . . of course," she replied.

She went into the office.

It was a large room in which there were a great number of tin boxes that contained the Estate-papers.

The walls were covered with maps of the large acreage owned by the Earl of Chadwood.

There were no fewer than eight villages and six farms besides the Home Farm which served Chad.

The woodlands were clearly marked.

There was also the lake, the streams which fed it, and a number of ponds and pools scattered amongst the farms.

Olivia sat down in a chair.

It was by the desk where Mr. Bentick kept a careful account of everything appertaining to the Estate.

On Fridays he distributed the wages earned by the indoor and outdoor staff.

Gerry stood in front of the maps, studying them.

Olivia thought he was comparing his debts with what his half-brother owned.

"What has happened, Mr. Bentick?" she asked in her soft voice. "I can see you are worried."

"Very worried, Miss Olivia! And as I do not know what to do, I am asking for your help."

"You know I will help if I can," Olivia answered.

Mr. Bentick produced a piece of paper which he handed across the desk.

She saw there were some names on it, and at the bottom was the Earl's signature.

"What is this?" she enquired.

"His Lordship informed me last night," Mr. Bentick replied, "that he has decided that no one under seventy will in future receive anything!"

"Nothing?" Olivia exclaimed.

"Nothing!" Mr. Bentick repeated. "That is a list of the pensioners in this village who are under seventy."

Olivia looked down at the paper and read the first name.

"But Mrs. Hunter is unable to work!" she exclaimed. "She cannot leave her cottage."

Mr. Bentick said nothing, and she went on:

"Mr. Walton is sixty-eight, and he has a very bad heart condition. The Doctor has told him that it is a mistake for him even to walk as far as the shops. What is he supposed to live on?"

Mr. Bentick did not answer, and she looked at the next name and read: "Mrs. Chapman—sixty-five."

"But she is . . . blind," she murmured, "almost. . . completely blind! Somebody always . . . fetches for her any . . . food she can . . . afford . . . to buy."

"I have told His Lordship this," Mr. Bentick said, "but he will not listen."

Olivia was still staring at the list.

"Mrs. Dunman is only sixty-one, but she has two grandchildren living with her because their parents are dead. If she cannot support them, and she is very ... frail, they will ... have to go into an ... Orphanage."

There was a break in her voice.

She recalled that was what the Earl had suggested should happen to Wendy.

There was one more name, Nick Howell—only forty-seven.

She stared at it, then she said:

"Surely you explained to His Lordship that Nick is a loon, as he has been ever since he was born. My father obtained a cottage for him because his family had no room for him in theirs."

"I know that, Miss Olivia, and he is quite harmless."

"Of course he is," Olivia agreed. "Even so ... he has to ... eat and he could ... no more earn any money ... than fly over ... the moon!"

She thought with a little constriction of her heart that the same could be said to apply to her.

Then she knew that she must not think of herself at the moment but try to help Mr. Bentick.

"What do you ... want me to do ... about this?" she asked.

She hoped he would not say "Speak to the Earl."

"I want you to tell the people what has happened," Mr. Bentick replied. "I cannot face them myself—I cannot—knowing they have been suffering for so long."

Olivia was very still.

Then she folded the list and put it into her pocket.

"I would like to think about it, Mr. Bentick," she said. "I want to help you, but I cannot quite see how I can do so."

"I understand, Miss Olivia," he said. "I know I

am being a coward, but having lived here for so long, I am fond of all those people, and I just cannot face them with this."

It was so unlike Mr. Bentick to be emotional in any way that Olivia knew he was really upset.

In a low voice she asked:

"Have you ... told the ... other villagers they are not to ... receive an ... increase in their ... reduced pensions?"

"I told two of them who called here for help," Mr. Bentick replied, "so I expect, by this time, they all know."

Olivia was well aware that the whole village would be concerned.

She rose to her feet and said to Gerry:

"We must go home ... after we have ... seen Mrs. Banks."

He looked at Mr. Bentick.

"Tell His Lordship I will not be here for luncheon, but will see him later in the afternoon."

"Very good, Mr. Gerald," Mr. Bentick replied. "This is a sad day, a very sad day for all of us."

Gerry drew some pieces of paper out of his pocket.

"This is what I came to see His Lordship about," he said, putting them down on the desk. "You might add them up and let me know the exact amount before I go back to London."

"You will be leaving to-morrow morning?" Mr. Bentick asked.

"I do not know," Gerry replied. "There is something I have to discuss first with Miss Olivia."

"I will put these in order for you, Mr. Gerald," Mr. Bentick said, picking up the papers.

Gerry took Olivia by the arm.

In silence they walked down the passage and through the baize door which led to the kitchen-quarters.

Upton was in the Pantry.

They could hear him talking sharply to one of the footmen.

They went into the huge kitchen which Olivia had always found fascinating when she was a child.

There was a small stove and a big one on which Mrs. Banks cooked for luncheons and dinner-parties and, when the late Earl had been well, for Banquets.

Olivia could remember as a child seeing Mrs. Banks make a huge iced cake.

It was a traditional part of the Christmas festivities at Chad.

There had been a three-tiered wedding-cake for one of the Cousins whom her Father had married at the Village Church.

Then there was a Birthday cake for her, for Tony, and for Wendy on every anniversary.

Mrs. Banks was a large, fat woman with cheeks like rosy apples.

She smiled when she saw who was entering her kitchen.

"It's nice to see you, Miss Olivia!" she said. "I've missed you since His Lordship arrived. And Mr. Gerald be quite a stranger!"

Gerald held out his hand.

"It would not be Chad without you here, Mrs. Banks!" he said. "Now I am going back to have luncheon with Miss Olivia, but she tells me she has nothing for me to eat."

Instead of looking surprised, Mrs. Banks said:

"I've 'eard 'bout your difficulties Miss Olivia, and it's that sorry I am. It'd shock th' old Earl, God rest 'im!"

Then, as if she could keep it to herself no longer, Mrs. Banks went on:

"It's not right, Mr. Gerald! It's not right! The things as is happenin' 'ere will make 'Is Lordship turn over in 'is grave!"

"What is happening?" Gerald asked.

"I'm told I'm to 'ave two women fewer in the kitchen an' there's to be only three housemaids upstairs besides two footmen instead of four!"

Olivia sat down on the nearest chair.

She knew without being told that all the servants who had been dismissed had been working at the Big House ever since they were twelve.

Now they were to be sent away for no good reason except that His Lordship was economising.

It was most unlikely that any of them would find work anywhere else in the neighbourhood.

"I've been 'ere over thirty years," Mrs. Banks was saying, "and I knows wots right and wots wrong! An' wot is 'appening now be wrong! There's no two ways about that!"

"I agree with you." Gerald said, "and I only wish there were something I could do."

"If Mr. William and Mr. John 'ad been spared, things'd be very different!" Mrs. Banks said bitterly.

Then, as if she forced herself to be practical, she said:

"Now, you wants somethin' for luncheon, an' that you shall 'ave. You run along 'ome, Miss Olivia, an'

35

take Master Tony with you. T'was all a mistake on the part of them London men who knows no better!"

"We will . . . go and set . . . him free," Olivia said in a weak voice.

"You do that," Mrs. Banks said, "and send young Bert in to me. 'E'll take your food down to Green Gables for you."

She looked at Gerald and gave him a smile.

"You'll not be going 'ungry, Mr. Gerald, not as long as I'm about.!"

"Thank you, Mrs. Banks," Gerald said, "and I have never forgotten the gingerbread biscuits you used to bake me to take back to School."

"Well, I expects you could still eat them now," Mrs. Banks said.

"I will not leave until I have tried them again!" Gerald promised.

As he helped Olivia from the chair, he said:

"Come along, Olivia, or our luncheon will arrive before we do."

"Thank you, Mrs. Banks," Olivia said. "I am sorry to bother you, but there really is very little in the house."

"I've heard as much, Miss Olivia," Mrs. Banks said, "and it be a cryin' shame, that's wot it is, seeing how much your Father an' your dear Mother did for everybody!"

Because Olivia felt like crying, she did not answer.

She only hurried Gerald away down the passage which led to the back-door.

They went out, and passing between the rhododendron bushes made their way to the stables.

As they neared them, to Olivia's surprise she heard laughter and the clapping of hands.

As the last of the bushes ended, they walked through an arched gateway.

In the cobbled yard they saw what was happening.

The grooms were all watching Tony.

He was giving a display on one of the older horses of what Olivia called his "Circus tricks."

She knew only too well how he could stand on a horse's back while it was trotting.

Then if they were on smooth ground he could put his head on the saddle with his legs in the air.

In the holidays he had been to every Circus in the vicinity.

He had learnt from them a great many other "tricks."

He could swing himself onto the ground while the horse was galloping, and back into the saddle without checking its pace.

He was always improving his skill.

Now Olivia saw that he was lying on his back with his legs over his head almost touching the horse's ears.

As he swung himself back into the saddle the stable-boys clapped and cheered.

Then when he saw Olivia he smiled at her and rode up at a gallop.

"Hello, Gerry!" he said. "Would you like to join me?"

"Not at the moment," Gerry replied. "We thought you would like to come home for luncheon."

"I am certainly hungry," Tony replied, "and I hope there is something other than rabbit to eat!"

"There is," Gerry replied, "but you had better hurry or we shall finish it before you get there."

Tony turned the horse round to ride it back to its stable.

As he did so, the Head Groom, who had been at Chad for years, came up to say:

"Sorry, Miss 'livia, 'bout Master Tony bein' brought 'ere by they foreigners from Lunnon! They tells 'Is Lordship 'bout 'im afore Oi 'ears it meself."

This was a grievance, Olivia knew.

She could not help smiling at the grooms from London being described as "foreigners."

But she was sure that was what they were to the people in the village.

"It seems, Graves." she said as she smiled, "that Master Tony's imprisonment has not been a very severe one!"

"Not when Oi learns where 'e'd bin put!" Graves said indignantly.

"I was going to ask you for a horse after luncheon," Gerry interposed. "But perhaps you could bring two to Green Gables for Mr. Tony and me,"

"Oi'll do that, Master Gerald," Graves said, "and it'll be th' two best in th' stable!"

"Thank you," Gerald said. "I shall look forward, as I always do, to riding anything you have."

Graves looked gratified.

Olivia and Gerald left the stable-yard and started to walk towards the lake.

They paused on the bridge, looking at the swans moving over the clear water.

The kingcups and the yellow irises were reflected in it.

At the far end there was the soft tinkle of the cascade as it fell over the rocks to a lower level.

"It is so . . . beautiful!" Olivia said. "How can he

live . . . here and be so . . . cruel?"

There was no need to say to whom she was referring, and Gerald said:

"I do not suppose the family have any idea yet of what he is like."

"Do you think he will . . . refuse to help . . . those who have always . . . depended . . . on Cousin Edward?" Olivia asked.

"I am quite certain of it," Gerry said. "What is he saving his money for, I would like to know! And there is a great deal of it!"

"He cannot do . . . this to the . . . pensioners!" Olivia said.

"I appreciate your thinking about them," Gerry said, "but first, Olivia, you have to think of yourself."

"I suppose there is no chance now of Tony going to Oxford!" Olivia murmured.

"If you want the truth—not a chance in Hell!"

"Then . . . what will . . . Tony do?"

"I am asking myself the same question," Gerry said.

She looked up at him as he spoke, and their eyes met.

It was obvious they were both thinking the same thing.

Gerry rested his arms on the balustrade of the bridge and bent forward.

"I am twenty-three," he said, "and I had no intention of marrying anybody—not for a long time. I suppose you feel the same."

"I thought perhaps . . . one day I would . . . fall in love . . . like Mama did when she was staying at Chad."

"Your Father was the best-looking man I have ever seen," Gerry said, "so it was not surprising!"

"Mama's parents were furious and wanted her to marry somebody much more important. But she told me that having seen Papa, there was for her no other man in the whole world."

"And that is what you hoped would happen to you," Gerry said.

"I am very fond of you, Gerry, you know that," Olivia said, "but I have always thought of you in the same way I thought of William and John, as if you were my brother."

"I suppose I felt the same," Gerry admitted. "If I am forced to marry at once, I would rather it was you than anybody else. At the same time, it is not right, is it?"

"No, of course it is not!" Olivia agreed. "But how can I . . . let Tony and Wendy . . . starve?"

She paused before she added:

" . . . or you go to prison!"

"How could we ever have guessed that he would be like this!" Gerry said violently. "Yet I suppose after hearing all the things my family said about his Mother, I might have suspected it."

"He has been a soldier," Olivia said, "so he is surely not still under her thumb?"

"She has been dead for three or four years," Gerry said, "but the poison with which she inoculated him has obviously gone deep!"

"I do not understand it," Olivia said. "I cannot understand any man being so unjust and . . . in a way . . . evil!"

"I am sorry, Olivia," Gerry murmured in a different tone. "Perhaps if I had not come here with

40

my debts he would at least have given you some money and somewhere to live, if it was only a cottage in the village."

Olivia shook her head.

"You must not blame yourself for that. He had already said no."

She drew in her breath before she said:

"He suggested that Tony could . . . work with horses . . . apparently as . . . a groom . . . and Wendy should go to an . . . Orphanage!"

Gerry stared at her. Then he said:

"Damn and blast him! He is intolerable! How dare he say anything like that to you!"

Olivia turned her face away.

"Let us go home," she said. "Cursing him is not going to help. He has the upper hand, and if we are to get any help from him, we will have to do what he wants."

"What he wants is wrong!" Gerry said. "I am sure that if your Father were alive, he would say that Good will always conquer Evil in the end!"

"We can only . . . pray," Olivia said simply.

"It is about the only thing we have left," Gerry agreed grimly.

Crossing the bridge, they began to walk through the Park under the oak trees.

Olivia was thinking how beautiful and peaceful it was, when suddenly in the distance they heard voices.

They were loud and noisy, and sounded as if a number of people were very angry.

Olivia stopped and put up her hand to touch Gerry's arm.

"What is happening?" she asked.

"I have no idea," he replied.

At that moment Olivia heard somebody running over the gravel onto the bridge.

She turned her head to see Tony coming towards them.

"Here I am!" he said. "You two have not got far!"

"We were just wondering." Olivia said, "what all this noise is about."

Tony stopped and listened.

As he did so, the voices seemed to grow still louder.

"It is a row of some sort," he said, "but I cannot think who is making it."

"Perhaps we had better go and find out?" Gerry suggested.

"Yes, of course." Olivia agreed.

They walked on.

Tony told them what had happened when the grooms seized him and said he was under arrest.

"For a moment I thought they must be joking," he said. "Then when I realised they were strange fellows I had never seen before, I explained who I was."

"What did they say to that?" Gerry asked.

"They would not listen. Just told me I was a thief and took me to the stables, where they shoved me into an empty stall and looked the stable-door!"

Olivia could not help smiling at the indignation in her brother's voice.

"It must have been very ignominious for you!" she sympathised. "But you are free now."

"I was free when Graves turned up, and he gave those London grooms a piece of his mind! I had to laugh at the expression on their faces!"

"Well, I have asked Graves to bring us some horses to Green Gables after luncheon," Gerry said. "With any luck, we will have a ride before His Lordship hears about it!"

"His Lordship?" Tony repeated. "Then you must have seen him, Olivia. What is he like?"

"I went to Chad to rescue you!" Olivia said.

She was just about to tell her brother how awful the Earl had been, when they passed through a clump of large oak trees.

They were then able to see a man who had his back to them with a number of village youths shouting at him.

They were screaming abuse at him, and now Olivia could hear one word quite clearly:

"Hungry! We be hungry!"

Now they could see that the man with his back to them was the Earl.

He was saying something they could not hear which brought forth a yell of anger and fury.

It was then Olivia was aware that something was lying on the ground over which the Earl and the youths were disputing.

With a little tremor she realised it was one of the spotted stags.

The youths must have killed it.

She suspected that two or three times in the last month deer had disappeared from the Park at night.

There was no evidence to substantiate her suspicions, but now the youths must have been caught red-handed.

She was certain the Earl was extremely angry.

Gerry and Tony were obviously thinking the same thing, but nobody moved.

Then suddenly one of the youths bent down and picked up a clod of earth and threw it at the Earl.

She heard him say something sharp and angry.

He raised the stick he was holding in his hand.

There were more clods of earth.

Then suddenly something flashed through the air and the Earl staggered backwards and fell to the ground.

Gerry and Tony started forward.

Even as they did so, the youths, and there were about a dozen of them, turned and ran.

By the time Gerry and Tony reached the Earl, he was lying on the ground beside the dead stag.

The handle of the knife with which he had been struck was protruding from his chest.

Olivia ran after the young men but could not catch up to them.

When she came back, Gerry was removing the long, sharp knife.

As he did so, the blood flowed from the wound in a crimson tide.

Olivia gave a little gasp of horror.

Going down on her knees, she put her hand on the Earl's forehead.

His eyes were closed, but he was alive and she thought quickly.

"It is too far to carry him back to Chad," she said. "We had better take him home, as it is so much nearer."

Fortunately the entrance to the garden was not more than thirty yards away.

They took the gate off its hinges, gently lifted

him onto it, and carried him slowly to the house.

Olivia ran ahead, opening the front-door and calling as she did so to Bessie.

She knew she would be there at this time of the morning.

Bessie was the one person in the village who would know what to do.

She not only nursed anyone who was ill, she was also the village Midwife, and laid out the dead.

"Bessie! Bessie!" Olivia called.

It was with a feeling of relief that she saw Bessie's kindly face looking over the bannisters.

"What is it, Miss Olivia?" she asked. "I hears as there were trouble up at t'Big House."

"It is the Earl!" Olivia said breathlessly. "He has been stabbed and he is bleeding fast. Mr. Gerry and Tony are bringing him here."

"Stabbed?" Bessie repeated in horror. "Whoever'd do such a terrible thing?"

Olivia did not reply.

She thought it would be a mistake for her to say it was youths from the village.

"We will put the Earl in Papa's bed-room," she said.

The bed was always made up just in case they had a stray visitor.

Sometimes Tony would bring one of his School-friends back with him unexpectedly.

"I'll open up t'room," Bessie said, "an' I'll want some hot water. There's a kettle on th' stove."

Olivia ran to the kitchen.

As she was waiting for the kettle to boil, she heard Gerry and Tony bringing the Earl into the house.

By the time she reached the hall, they were carrying him up the stairs on the gate.

Bessie was giving instructions as to how careful they should be.

They took the Earl into the bed-room which had been occupied by her Father and Mother.

There was a dust-sheet on the bed, and very gently they transferred him from the gate onto it.

There were also towels and a bowl.

She was not surprised to see Bessie produce a large cardboard box.

Her mother had always kept it ready for accidents, and it contained lint and bandages.

"Now, listen, Master Tony," Bessie said briskly, "you go off for t'Doctor while I do the best I can to clean the wound and stop the bleeding."

She looked round and saw that Olivia was standing just inside the door and added:

"Please, Miss Olivia, go down and get the hot water."

Olivia did as she was told, appreciating before she left the room how Bessie was deftly unbuttoning the Earl's coat and his shirt.

"How can this have happened?" Olivia asked herself as she ran down the stairs. "Perhaps when he is better he will punish the whole village in some horrible manner!"

She was frightened at the thought of what would be the villagers' reaction.

When she reached the kitchen she found Bert there with a hamper he had brought from Mrs. Banks.

"T'were reel 'eavy, Miss 'livia," he said, "but Oi managed it!"

"That was splendid of you, Bert!"

Olivia wondered if she should tell him that the Earl had been injured.

Then she thought it would be a mistake.

Instead, she gave him twopence from her almost empty purse.

He went off happily to spend the money on sweets at the village shop.

The kettle was not yet boiling.

Olivia opened the hamper to find that Mrs. Banks had certainly kept her word.

There were two chickens already plucked and trussed, a ham, and an ox tongue which had been cooked but not yet carved.

There was a dish containing Mrs. Banks's Duck Pâté, eggs, cheese, newly baked bread, butter, and a pudding.

It was wonderful to see so much delicious food after weeks of eating nothing but rabbit.

She forgot everything for the moment.

To-day, at any rate, Tony and Wendy would not go hungry.

Then she told herself she should not be worrying about anything except the Earl.

She picked up the kettle which was now boiling and went upstairs.

She knocked on the door.

"Wait a minute!" Bessie called.

Olivia waited.

She was thinking that of all the people in the world she would have been willing to have as a guest, the last person she wanted in Green Gables was the Earl.

She hated him.

She hated anybody who could be so cruel, so unkind, and completely heartless, not only to her, but to the old people in the village, and particularly the five he had selected to have to wait until they were seventy before they could have any money.

It shot through her mind that if he died, Gerry would take his place.

Then she told herself it was wrong and wicked to wish anyone dead.

Her Father would have been shocked.

"I must pray for his recovery," she told herself.

At the same time, she was well aware that it would be a hard thing for her to do.

How could she pray for a man who intended to force her into marriage with a man she did not love and who did not love her.

"Until death us do part."

She could hear her voice making the vow.

"I cannot do it!" she said out loud.

chapter three

IT was two o'clock before they ate the luncheon which Mrs. Banks had sent for them.

The Doctor had come.

He said it was a miracle that the point of the knife had not pierced the Earl's heart.

If it had, he would have been dead.

As it was, he had to keep completely still so as not to lose any more blood.

Therefore, the longer he remained unconscious, the better.

"When he wakes up," Dr. Emmerson, who had looked after Olivia and her brother and sister since they were born, said, "I could give him something to make him sleep, but your Mother's herbs would be better."

He smiled as he spoke.

Olivia knew he had always encouraged the villagers to cure their illnesses with the herbs her Mother grew in the garden.

"I have all Mama's recipes," Olivia told him, "so

I can make a sleeping-draught exactly as she did."

"He could not be in better hands than yours and Bessie's," the Doctor said. "I will call this evening, and again to-morrow morning. Quite frankly, Olivia, there is little else we can do."

He reached the door before he said:

"I suppose it would be better not to ask how His Lordship got injured in this way?"

"Much better!" Olivia replied. "Gerry, Tony, and I were too far . . . away to recognise or . . . identify . . . anyone."

The Doctor smiled and put his hand on her shoulder.

"You are a wise girl, Olivia," he said, "and you champion the village in the same way as your Father always did."

Olivia was about to tell him how unsuccessful she had been with the Earl.

Then she thought there was no point in doing so at this moment.

She also realised the family were waiting for luncheon and Bessie had it ready.

"Let us eat," she said as soon as the Doctor had left, "and then we must decide what we are going to do."

She was speaking to Gerry, and Tony asked:

"What do you mean by that?"

"I will tell you later," Olivia replied evasively.

She did not want to say anything while Wendy was there.

The child was already dancing round the Dining-Room, thrilled with the food laid out on the table.

She had been having lessons all the morning with

a retired Governess who came every day to teach her.

Miss Davison was a very nice woman.

When Olivia explained shyly that they could no longer afford to pay her, she had merely said:

"I enjoy teaching Wendy. She is a very intelligent little girl, and from what you are telling me, Miss Olivia, she will need her brains in the future."

"We will all . . . need . . . them," Olivia said in a low voice, knowing how little money they had left.

Now, as they entered the Dining-Room, Wendy was saying:

"Look at all the luscious things Mrs. Banks has sent for us to eat! I'se hungry, wery, wery hungry!"

"So am I," Tony admitted. "After all the dramatics of this morning, I could eat an ox!"

"Start with what we have here!" Olivia said as she smiled. "And personally, I want some of Mrs. Banks's delicious duck pâté."

They all enjoyed that.

As there had been no time to cook anything, they ate the tongue and the ham.

Bessie had already prepared some vegetables before they had come in with the Earl.

Afterwards there was one of Mrs. Banks's most elaborate puddings made from spongecake and cream.

The four of them finished the whole dish.

Having been on such short rations for so long, Olivia found she could not eat any more.

But Tony and Gerry finished the meal with cheese.

Then there was coffee, which Mrs. Banks had included in the hamper.

Tony sat back in his chair and said:

"I feel like a different man!"

"Try not to do anything crazy this afternoon," Olivia said, "because we have all got to take it in turns to look after the Earl."

Gerry gave an exclamation.

"I know what we will do," he said, "and I should have thought of it before!"

"What is that?" Tony asked.

"We can ask Bentick and Upton to take turns in looking after him," Gerry replied.

"I think his Valet would be better," Olivia said.

"Shall we send up to the House, or shall I go myself?" Gerry asked.

Then, as he realised he had a great deal to say to Olivia, he added:

"Unless you will go for me, Tony?"

"Of course I will," Tony said. "But do not forget that Graves is bringing us some horses to ride in a few minutes."

"That will certainly make things easier," Gerry agreed.

As he spoke, there was a knock on the front-door.

"I expect that is Graves," Olivia said, "although I did not hear any horses arriving."

She went from the Dining-Room as she spoke and opened the door.

It was Ted who stood there.

"Oi thinks ye ought t'know, Miss 'livia," he said, "there be real trouble 'appening on t'Green!"

"What sort of trouble?" Olivia enquired.

She was aware as she spoke that Tony and Gerry had come out of the Dining-Room and were just behind her.

"They be roastin' a stag, Miss 'livia," Ted said, "an' sayin' 'cause 'Is Lordship's threatens to 'ave t'em deported, they're gonna burn down t'Big 'ouse!"

Olivia gave a cry of horror.

"They . . . cannot do . . . that!"

"That's wot they says," Ted affirmed, "an' they be real wild, as be th' pensioners!"

"Are they on the Green too?" Olivia asked.

"A 'ole lot o' them be," Ted replied. "They be shakin' their fists an' sayin' as th' Earl's a-tryin' t'kill them!"

There was silence for a moment.

Then Olivia said to Gerry:

"We have to do something, and quickly!"

"What can we do?" he asked.

Olivia turned to Ted.

"Listen, Ted," she said, "run as fast as you can up to the House and ask Mr. Bentick to come here immediately and bring all the money he has with him. Tell him what has happened, and tell Mr. Upton too."

"Oi'll do that, Miss 'livia," Ted agreed.

He was obviously delighted at being in the important position of "first with the news."

He ran across the garden and let himself out into the Park.

Wendy ran a little way after him, and the three others looked at each other in consternation.

"We have to do something to stop this!" Olivia said.

"I cannot think Bentick will have enough ready money to be of much help," Gerry remarked. "And anyway, he will be reluctant to part with it. You know as well as I do that, if he does, Lenox will dismiss him when he recovers."

There was silence.

Then Olivia said:

"As the Earl is unconscious, he can do nothing about what is happening. It is now your responsibility."

"Why mine?" Gerry asked.

"You are his Heir Presumptive," Olivia pointed out.

He stared at her in astonishment before he said:

"I suppose I am, but actually I never thought of it!"

"Then, as you are his heir," Tony said, "you have to show some authority and at least stop them from burning down the House."

His voice rose almost to a cry as he added:

"They might hurt the horses! I must warn Graves!"

"Wait a minute!" Olivia said. "We have to think how Gerry can explain and make the people believe that now, until the Earl recovers, he is in charge."

She looked at Gerry as she said:

"They know they can trust you."

"That will not be much help," he said roughly, "if I cannot give them any money. As it is, I will soon be taken off to prison because I cannot pay my debts."

There was silence.

Then Olivia said as if she were trying to find her way out of a maze:

"If Cousin Edward were too ill to give any orders when he was dying, who was in a position to pay out the money for those who were working in the House and on the Estate?"

"He would have given somebody Power of Attorney," Gerry replied.

Olivia looked bewildered, and he explained:

"It means that somebody else would have authority to sign cheques and give orders, and everything would go on as usual."

"What does a Power of Attorney look like?" Olivia enquired.

As if he thought it a pointless question, Gerry replied casually:

"Oh, it would be just a piece of paper signed with Cousin Edward's name."

As he spoke, he was suddenly still.

He looked at Olivia, and they were both thinking the same thing.

Slowly, as if she were afraid of what she was doing, she put her hand into her pocket.

She drew out the piece of paper which Mr. Bentick had given her with the names of the five villagers on it who were no longer entitled to a pension.

At the bottom there was Earl's signature:

"Chadwood"

Gerry stared at it.

Then, after what seemed like a long silence, he said:

"Do you really think we can do it?"

"We have to!" Olivia said. "We cannot allow Chad to be burnt to the ground, nor can we let everybody go on starving."

"That is true!" Tony, who was listening, said. "I told you I felt like a different man once I had had something decent to eat. Those wretched people in the village have not had a square meal since Cousin Edward died."

"I will write . . . down what the . . . form should . . . say," Olivia said in a very low voice to Gerry, "then we will . . . have to . . . obtain his . . . signature."

"It will need two witnesses."

"Tony and I will be witnesses," Olivia answered, "and if we end up in prison, then at least we will all be together!"

Gerry did not say any more.

He sat down at the writing-desk and took a piece of paper with the address printed on it from the holder.

He wrote the date at the top. Then underneath he put:

"Having been injured and feeling extremely ill, I give my half-brother, Gerald Wood, Power of Attorney until I have recovered."

Gerry waited for the ink to dry.

Then he held out the piece of paper to Olivia.

Taking it, she said:

"Both of you follow me, and bring the pen and ink with you."

They went upstairs.

At least she thought they would not lie any more than was absolutely necessary.

It was wrong to do so—of course it was wrong.

As she reached her Father's bed-room, she said in her heart:

"Forgive me . . . Papa . . . but you know . . . there is . . . nothing else we . . . can do."

She had the feeling that her Father understood.

They walked into the bed-room and instinctively they all moved on tip-toe.

Bessie had drawn the blinds half-way down.

Nevertheless, it was easy to see the Earl lying on his back with his eyes closed.

His face was very pale.

For one moment Olivia thought he must be dead.

Then she touched his hand.

He was alive, but completely unconscious.

She picked up a book from the side-table.

Laying it on the bed, she placed the piece of paper on top of it.

Then she handed Tony the list on which there was the Earl's signature.

He understood that she wanted him to hold it so that she could see it clearly.

Gerry dipped the pen in the ink.

Somehow she managed to place the Earl's fingers on each side of it.

Then she held his hand with both of hers.

She copied his signature near enough to the one he had done himself to be credible.

It was slightly shaky, but that would be understandable in the circumstances.

Then she put down the Earl's hand and replaced the book before they all left the room.

They had not spoken one word since they had entered it.

They went down again to the Study.

Olivia signed her name at the bottom of the paper, and Tony added his.

When it was done, Olivia spoke for the first time.

"Now we have to go to the Village Green!" she said.

"The horses are here," Gerry told her, "and I suggest we all ride."

"That is a good idea," Tony agreed. "It will certainly look more impressive."

Olivia went to the front-door.

She opened it and saw that outside Graves was riding one horse and a groom was on each of the others.

Before she could speak, Gerry walked past her to say:

"There is some trouble, Graves, on the Green, and we are going to see what can be done about it. Put a side-saddle on one of the horses for Miss Olivia."

"Oi'll do that, Mr. Gerald," Graves said, "an' Oi 'ears things be in a bad way, which ain't surprising."

Because Gerry had said she was to ride, Olivia ran upstairs to put on her bonnet.

There was no time for her to change into her riding-habit.

Anyway, when they had horses of their own, she often jumped on the back of one just wearing her ordinary gown to go to the village or in the Park.

She came down the stairs wearing her pretty bonnet trimmed with cornflowers.

Bessie was coming from the kitchen.

"Where you be off to, Miss 'livia?" she asked.

"We are going to try and stop the trouble on the

Green," Olivia replied. "Will you please look after His Lordship? Ted has gone to Chad to ask for his Valet to come and help us."

"That be sensible!" Bessie said approvingly.

"Wendy will stay here with you," Olivia said.

But when she went outside she saw that Wendy was sitting at the front of Tony's saddle.

There was a side-saddle on the horse which Graves had been riding.

As he helped her to mount, she said to Gerry:

"Perhaps it is a mistake for Wendy to come with us in case she is hurt."

"Unless this village has gone completely crazy," Gerry replied, "there is no reason why anybody should hurt Wendy, or any of us, for that matter."

He grinned before he finished:

"They might take a swipe at me, I suppose, because I am Lenox's half-brother!"

"You will not forget the pensioners," Olivia said.

"You will have to help me," he answered. "Stand beside me and prompt me. I have never played at being an Earl before."

Because he spoke with a hint of amusement in his voice, Olivia could not help giving a little chuckle.

As Gerry had said, the whole thing was mad.

It did not seem possible they were not taking part in a drama at the Playhouse.

They rode off slowly.

Olivia was trying frantically to think of everything Gerry should say.

At the same time, she was terrified that the villagers would not listen to him.

Perhaps they would throw things at him as they had at the Earl.

It was comforting to know that Graves and the two grooms were just behind them.

They were walking as quickly as they were riding.

As they neared the Green, it was obvious from the noise that everything was in a tumult.

One glance told Olivia that practically everyone in the village was there.

They were all talking in high, excited voices.

From a corner of the Green came the smell of roasting venison.

As they drew nearer, Olivia could see the stag which was hung over the leaping flames of a wood fire.

She recognised the youths crouching round it as those who had attacked the Earl.

Even before the stag was properly cooked she could see them tearing pieces of flesh off it.

She knew they were hungry and, being young, had been driven to breaking-point.

There had been no work for them.

They and their families had subsisted on vegetables which they stole from the fields and the rabbits and birds they trapped.

Then, as they rode nearer still and the horses reached the Green, there was a sudden silence.

Everybody stared at them.

Olivia realised Tony had been clever in advising they should arrive on horseback rather than on foot.

She had a feeling that if they had walked even half-way up the Green, they would have been surrounded.

Everyone would have been trying to tell them their grievances.

It would have been difficult if not impossible to proceed any further.

Gerry, however, knew exactly what he intended to do.

He rode straight to the Inn called the Dog and Duck.

In front of it there was a long, heavy wooden table made from the trunk of a tree.

It was here the older inhabitants sat in the evenings.

If they had any money, they drank ale or home-made cider from large pewter mugs.

When he reached the table, Gerry dismounted and helped Olivia down from her horse and lifted her onto the table.

The grooms, who were just behind them, took the horses by their bridles and led them away.

Then Tony and Wendy sat down on a wooden bench behind them.

Olivia and Gerry just stood looking at the crowd.

Then, as the people began to surge round them, Gerry said in a loud, penetrating voice:

"Will you all come as near to me as possible, because I have something of importance to say to you."

There was a murmur which Olivia realised was half interest and half anger.

She knew from the expression on the faces which were so familiar to her that the younger people were feeling aggressive.

The older ones appeared helpless, as if many of them might collapse.

However, because they were curious, even the youths round the roasting stag left it.

They stood on the outskirts of the crowd, looking hostile.

"First of all," Gerry began, "you have known me since I was a child. I have always been happy at Chad, and that is what I want to feel again."

"Ye'll never be that as long as that new Earl's a-livin' there!" somebody shouted.

"I am here to-day," Gerry said, ignoring the interruption, "to tell you that my half-brother has been injured and is desperately ill."

There was silence.

Olivia saw the youths who had assaulted him look at each other uncomfortably.

"He has therefore asked me to take his place," Gerry was saying, "until he is better. I need your help in order to get things going and make Chad the happy place it was when the late Earl was alive."

"T'were a different place then!" somebody shouted. "Not t'hell it be now!"

"If it is a hell," Gerry retorted, "then you will have to help me to change it back into the Heaven I remember."

"Ye can't do that wi'out spendin' money!" the same man shouted.

"There I agree with you," Gerry said, "so will you all listen very carefully to what I want you to do."

There was a hush as they waited, and Gerry said:

"First, will everybody who worked in the House and on the Estate before my Cousin died please return to their jobs immediately! In the house every department needs increasing, with footmen, housemaids, and those in the kitchen."

He smiled before he added:

"You know Mrs. Banks never has enough help!"

There was a small wave of laughter at this, and Gerry went on:

"Outside, we are short of gardeners, game-keepers, wood-cutters, and I am quite certain Graves will need more lads in the stables."

Olivia glanced at Graves and saw the astonishment on his face.

Standing beside him were Mr. Bentick and Upton, who were staring at Gerry as if they thought he had gone mad.

"Now we come to the village," Gerry continued, "and the first thing Miss Olivia has told me to tell you is that the pensions of the retired people will be doubled from to-day!"

The pensioners stiffened and, speaking to them, he said:

"All the money that was withheld from you last year before the Earl reached England will be refunded to you in cash."

For a moment there was just a gasp of surprise.

Then there were cheers which seemed to echo round the Green.

Olivia saw that one or two of the older people had tears running down their cheeks.

"Next," Gerry said when he could make himself heard, "Miss Olivia has given me two ideas as to how everybody in this village can be employed and earn good money."

He paused before saying slowly:

"Her first idea is that we should re-open the Slate Mine."

He looked about him, and Olivia murmured:

"Mr. Cutler."

"Is Mr. Cutler here?" Gerry asked.

A middle-aged man held up his hand.

"I think, Mr. Cutler," Gerry said, "you managed at the Slate Mine when it was open?"

"That Oi did, Sir," Mr. Cutler agreed, "an' we was a-doin' fine 'til it were shut down."

"I understand now that slate is very much in demand." Gerry said, "and I want you to employ as many men as possible and get the Mine going again."

"Do ye mean that?" Mr. Cutler asked in amazement.

"You can fix it up with Mr. Bentick, who is here, and I suggest you start at once! To-day, or, better still, yesterday!"

There was faint laughter at this.

Olivia could see the villagers were stunned, as if they could not believe what they were hearing.

"And now," Gerry said, "I want your help on another very important matter."

He glanced at Olivia as he spoke, and she said:

"Temple . . . Mr. Temple!"

"Where is Mr. Temple?" Gerry shouted. "I hope he is here, because I need him badly."

An intelligent-looking man of forty-five to fifty years pushed his way to the front.

"Oi be 'ere, Mr. Gerald," he said.

"Good!" Gerry said. "Now, Mr. Temple, I want you to start at once with the largest team of men and boys you can muster to repair first all the pensioners' cottages, then all the other cottages in the village, and finally the old Vicarage."

"The old Vicarage?" Mr. Temple repeated.

"If you want a new Vicar, and do not want to turn Miss Olivia out of Green Gables, it has to be made into a decent place in which to live,—within a few weeks!"

Mr. Temple nodded his head.

"Oi'll do me best, Mr. Gerald," he said, "but it's a tall order, an' no mistake!"

"But not for you, and with all the able-bodied men I see here to give you a hand!" Gerry said.

Then people began to talk with sheer excitement, and Gerry said:

"One minute! I realise that all this is going to need a great deal of strength and vigour. But owing to the unfortunate circumstances of last year, when things went wrong, you are none of you as strong as you should be."

"Not wi' empty bellies!" someone shouted.

"That is true," Gerry agreed, "and that is why I want to speak to Mr. Bolton."

Olivia had just whispered the name of the Butcher.

A large, red-faced man pushed his way to the front of those who were listening.

"Oi be 'ere, Sir," he said to Gerry.

"And I am delighted to see you!" Gerry said. "Now, Mr. Bolton, you have to make all these people strong enough to transform the village into a happy place again, and that means they need food."

Mr. Bolton waited expectantly.

"For the next week, or until they get their wages," Gerry said, "I am asking you to provide every family in the village with a large joint a day of beef or mutton."

There was a cry of excitement.

Then everybody was shouting and clapping.

When he could make himself heard, Gerry said:

"Mr. Trueman, who bakes better than any other Baker I know, will provide enough loaves of his bread for every man, woman, and child to have all they want, and Mr. Geary will give each family a pound of butter and enough cheese to fill in the gaps which Mr. Bolton has left empty."

The villagers were chattering with excitement like magpies, and Gerry said:

"One more thing. I shall need somebody to arrange that every child up to the age of ten has a pint of milk every day from one of the Farms. I am sure I can leave that in the hands of some of the Mothers here."

He paused before he added:

"If there are any difficulties, if there is anything I have forgotten, I shall be at Chad, and Miss Olivia will be at Green Gables. I promise you we will both do all we can to make you as happy as you ought to be."

He looked at the crowd before he added:

"And let me say how much I admire you all for your courage and endurance over the past year. We can only pray that this sort of thing will never happen again."

It was then that the people went mad.

The men threw their caps in the air, the women wiped their eyes and clapped, and Gerry and Olivia got down off the table.

Everybody wanted to shake hands with them.

There were tears in Olivia's eyes as she took Wendy by the hand and moved amongst the old people.

"Be it true, Miss 'livia?" they kept asking. "We was told 'Is Lordship said we couldn't have no more money than wot we had last year."

"It was all a mistake," Olivia said, "and do not think about it any more."

"Oi be a-thinkin' it'll be noice t'have me roof mended!" one woman said. "It's bin leakin' somethin' terrible when it rains!"

Another clasped Olivia's hand and said:

"Oi knows as it's all due to ye, Miss 'livia, Dearie. 'Tis as if yer dear Mother 'as come down from Heaven to 'elp us."

"I am sure she has," Olivia said.

She turned to find herself facing Mr. Bentick.

He looked more worried than usual, and he said to her in a low voice which only she could hear:

"Is it true, Miss Olivia? Mr. Gerald has just told me he has Power of Attorney. But what will His Lordship say when he finds out how much has been spent?"

"He is very ill at the moment, and unconscious," Olivia explained, "and we had to do something! The people in the village were threatening to burn down the House! At least Mr. Gerald has prevented that from happening."

"Burn down the House?" Mr. Bentick exclaimed in horror.

"That is what would have happened if Mr. Gerald had not done what ought to have been done a long time ago."

It was nearly an hour before they could ride their horses back to Green Gables.

Graves followed behind them.

He had a crowd of youths begging him to give

them employment in the stables.

When they reached Green Gables, the youths remained outside the gate.

Graves said to Gerry:

"Oi s'pose, Mr. Gerald, ye realise we need some more 'orses? Most o' those in t'stables be gettin' old."

"I am aware of that," Gerry said, "and Mr. Tony and I will buy some new ones at the first opportunity we can go to Tattersall's."

"There be a good 'Orse Fair in Oxford next week," Graves said optimistically.

"Then we will attend it, and you shall come with us," Gerry promised.

The smile on Graves's face was thanks enough.

Gerry had dismounted while he was talking.

Now he said, as Olivia was going into the house:

"I am going to Chad. Is there anything you want?"

Olivia paused.

"I can think of a lot of things," she replied, "but perhaps it would be wrong to ask for them."

"Then leave it to me," Gerry said. "I will bring some food for dinner, because I am dining with you, and Upton and the footmen can wait on us."

Olivia's eyes lit up as he remounted.

Then she walked to his horse and stood looking up at him.

"Can we really do things like that?" she asked little above a whisper.

"We have done so much already that a little more is of no consequence," Gerry answered. "I intend to get Bentick to pay my debts and double the allowance your Mother had before she died."

"You . . . you cannot . . . do that!" Olivia exclaimed.

"You forget—I have Power of Attorney and can therefore do anything!"

He smiled at her, swept off his hat, then rode towards the gate that led into the Park.

Tony followed him, and so did Graves on the horse Olivia had been riding.

Feeling as if the whole world had turned topsy-turvy, she went into the house.

As Wendy ran into the kitchen to find Bessie, Olivia went up the stairs.

She opened the door into the Earl's room.

He was still lying as she had last seen him, and his eyes were closed.

But also in the room sitting by the window was a man she realised must be his Valet.

She stood for a moment looking down at the Earl, thinking he looked even paler than when she had last seen him.

As she left the room, the Valet followed her.

Outside, Olivia held out her hand and said:

"You must be Higgins, His Lordship's Valet."

"That's right, Miss," Higgins replied, "an' I come soon as I were told what 'ad 'appened."

"The Doctor says His Lordship is not to be moved in any circumstances, but I would be very grateful if you could help Bessie and me nurse him."

" 'Course I will!" Higgins said as he grinned. "I've bin 'Is Lordship's batman ever since 'e joined the Regiment an' us 'ave bin in some tight corners afore now."

"You mean when you were fighting?" Olivia asked, wondering who the enemy had been.

69

"Us were out in India," Higgins explained, "an' 'Is Lordship were always in th' thick o' things, one way or another!"

From the way he spoke it was obvious that if no one else admired the new Earl, his Valet did.

Olivia could not help remembering that somebody had once said that "no man was a hero to his Valet."

It made her think that perhaps the Earl had hidden qualities they had not yet discovered.

For the moment, however, she was more concerned with practicalities.

"I think it is important that you should have a room as close as possible to His Lordship, and there is a Dressing-Room next door."

It was the room in which her Father had kept his clothes.

One wall was covered with a huge wardrobe.

But there was a small bed which she could never remember being used.

"That'll suit me fine, Miss," Higgins said, "an' don't you worry 'bout me. I'm used to roughing it, so to speak. An' it'll make His Lordship feel at home, if it comes to that!"

Olivia laughed.

"I hope he will be comfortable here, and if there is anything you want, please ask for it."

"I'll do that," Higgins assured her, "an' thanks very much, Miss."

He went back into the Earl's room, and Olivia went downstairs.

Bessie was in the kitchen, and as Olivia entered she guessed the chickens were roasting.

"At least we have something for dinner," she

70

said, "and I am sure Mr. Gerry will be sending down some more food."

"We'll need it with 'Is Lordship and his Valet stayin'!" Bessie remarked. "But Mrs. Banks won't forget us."

Wendy, who was sitting at the kitchen-table, got up to slip her hand into Olivia's.

"Can I'se go and look at the man who's in Dadda's bed-room?" she asked.

Olivia shook her head.

"No, darling, he is very ill. What I want you to do is to come with me into the garden to find some of Mama's herbs to help make him well again."

"They'll do that 'cos they are magic!" Wendy said.

Olivia did not reply.

She could not help feeling that the longer the Earl was unconscious, the better it would be for the village as well as for Gerry and herself.

She did not dare to think of what would happen when he found out what they had done, or counted up the money they had spent!

"Whatever happens," she told herself, "at least to-morrow, if not to-night, no one will go hungry. Also, if all the repairs are done before he can stop the men from working, they will have earned enough to feel proud of themselves again."

She was frightened of her own thoughts, and of the future.

As she picked the herbs to make the medicine which the villagers believed had a special White Magic, she was praying.

"Please God . . . please . . . do not let him . . . get well . . . too quickly."

chapter four

GERRY came into the Sitting-Room where Olivia was waiting for him.

He was in his riding-clothes and appeared to be bursting with good health.

"Good-morning, Olivia!" he said. "You were asleep when I came for breakfast. Did Lenox have a good night?"

"Much better," Olivia answered, "and the Doctor has been here and says he is very pleased with him."

She had taken it in turns with Higgins to nurse the Earl, but the last ten days had been very difficult.

He had run a very high temperature from his injury, and they had to prevent him from throwing himself about or turning over.

'It is due to Mama's herbs,' Olivia thought, 'that the wound is healing day by day.'

Bessie had offered to do one shift with them, but

she had so much to do in the daytime that Olivia had refused.

Olivia stayed with the Earl for the first part of each night.

At two o'clock in the morning Higgins took over from her.

Now, having slept until ten o'clock, Olivia felt rested.

She was looking better and not so thin as she had done previously.

Gerry crossed the room, and going to the grog-tray, poured himself a glass of sherry.

"How can you have done anything so outrageous," she asked, "as to order me those new gowns?"

When Olivia had woken, she had found to her astonishment several large dress-boxes outside her bed-room door.

When she opened them, she saw they contained new gowns!

They were far more beautiful, and certainly more expensive, than anything she had ever owned before.

"It is only what you deserve," Gerry said, "and Bessie gave me one of your old gowns, so they ought to fit you like a glove."

"They are perfect!" Olivia replied. "And I hope you admire the one I am wearing."

"You look very lovely," Gerry assured her, "but then, you always do!"

"At the same time," Olivia said in a low voice, "you must not spend money on things that are just sheer extravagance!"

Gerry sat down in one of the arm-chairs.

"I have worked it out like this," he said. "When Lenox recovers, he is certain, unless he has changed considerably, to cancel everything I have done. So we might as well enjoy ourselves while we can, and be sensible enough to put a little bit by for the future."

"I am ... sure that is ... something we should ... not do," Olivia protested.

"It is what I intend to do where you are concerned," Gerry replied, "and I have done something else of which I hope you will approve."

"What is that?"

"I have written to Oxford and paid Tony's fees for his first term at Magdalen."

Olivia gave a cry.

"But ... Gerry ... that is ... stealing! The Earl is certain to ... ask for it back."

"I doubt it," Gerry replied. "It would make him look a fool and proclaim to the world how mean he is."

There was silence, Then Olivia said:

"I ... I do not ... know what to ... say or ... what to ... do."

"Then just leave everything to me," Gerry said, "and, incidentally, I am enjoying myself. I have seen Farmer Hampton this morning, and he is absolutely delighted with the improvements I suggested for his Farm, which of course I will pay for."

Olivia made a little murmur, but she knew it was useless to argue with Gerry.

In the last two weeks he had spent money in a manner which she knew would horrify the Earl when he discovered it.

It would doubtless bring a terrible retribution on their heads.

Only yesterday he and Tony had come back to announce that they had bought two more excellent horses, and that was on top of the ones they had bought at the Oxford Horse Fair.

When she expostulated, Gerry had said:

"If William had been alive, they are exactly what he would have bought, and the stables, as we all know, have run down a great deal since Cousin Edward became ill and there was no one to give orders."

"But . . . what will the Earl . . . say?" Olivia asked in a frightened voice.

"He ought to be pleased at having some extremely fine horses at what actually were reasonable prices." Gerry replied.

As he finished his glass of wine, he said:

"I know I am being wildly extravagant, but it is not the same as the extravagance in which I indulged in London. Everything I have done here has been for the good of the Estate and to help the people on it."

"I know that," Olivia replied, "but my . . . gowns . . ."

"You come into the same category," Gerry interrupted, "you are part of the family and part of the Estate. I can hardly ride new horses while you go around dressed in rags like a Gypsy!"

Olivia laughed.

At the same time, she could understand Gerry's somewhat twisted logic.

The only thing was that she hardly dared to think of the future, or how angry the Earl would be.

When she looked at him lying in bed, white-cheeked and unconscious, he did not seem so terrifying.

In fact, she forgot how unpleasant he had been, and how much she had hated him.

Instead, he was just a young man who was ill and suffering.

In some ways he was like a small boy who had been injured accidentally.

When she talked to Higgins she began to understand why he was as he was.

"I been with His Lordship since he first joined th' Regiment," he said, "an' as we was stationed 'ere in England, 'e used t'go 'ome regularly."

"Tell me what it is like," Olivia asked.

She could not help being curious, because the two brothers were so utterly different from each other.

"If ever there was a dragon o' a woman," Higgins answered, "t'were His Lordship's Mother! Suspicious wasn't the word for it: Her thought everyone was a criminal an' her were just waitin' to catch 'em out!"

"Why should she be like that?" Olivia asked.

Higgins shrugged his shoulders.

"Search me!" he said. "T'were just 'er nasty mind, an' her drove everyone as served 'er mad!"

"In what way?" Olivia asked.

She knew it was wrong to question Higgins about the Earl's private life.

Yet she wanted to understand what made him behave in such a cruel and unkind way.

"They used t'say in the kitchen as her counted the crumbs as they fell off the bread, an' measured every drop o' milk as comes from th' cow!"

Olivia laughed.

"Her were!" Higgins asserted. "I could hear her telling His Lordship, Mr. Lenox, as he be then, how terrible everyone was an' 'ow they was a-pickin' 'is pocket every time 'e turned 'is back on 'em!"

"What made her so unpleasant?" Olivia asked.

"I suppose her thinks as 'er had been unhappy with one man, 'er had to take 'er revenge on all the rest!"

Olivia sat by the Earl's bed-side that night, rising to hold him if he made the slightest movement.

She wondered, when he was still, how he had allowed himself to be so much influenced by his Mother.

She had made him believe that everybody was against him.

But surely in his Regiment everything was different?

She had not had a chance of talking about that to Higgins.

Then, yesterday, when they were waiting for the Doctor to arrive, she had asked:

"Did the soldiers who served under His Lordship like him?"

Higgins considered this for a moment.

"They be afraid of him," he said, "but they admired him. We couldn't help it."

"What exactly did you admire him for?" Olivia enquired.

"He were that brave, and afore we left India he were a hero!"

"A hero!" Olivia repeated in astonishment.

"He saved the lives of two of our men when they'd

fallen into enemy hands," Higgins said, "and under his leadership, the troops as he commanded was always called 'The Tigers!' "

"Because they were so ferocious?" Olivia asked.

"That's the reason, right enough," Higgins said as he grinned, "and whatever us undertook we were never defeated!"

Olivia thought that was why the Earl expected everybody to obey his commands and would listen to no arguments.

She knew from other things Higgins told her why the men who had served under him admired him.

But they did not love him as the villagers had loved William and John, nor in the way they had adored her Mother.

Now, as Gerry watched the expression on her face, he said gently:

"Stop worrying, Olivia, and just enjoy to-day. To-morrow may never come!"

"That is a dismal way to think," Olivia replied.

"Not as dismal as your fussing yourself stupid as to what Lenox will say when he is on his feet again. Let us wait until he is, but at the same time be prepared."

Olivia did not answer, and after a moment he said:

"That reminds me—you must go and look at the Vicarage. They have worked marvels on it already!"

"Bessie has been telling me about that," Olivia said.

"I wonder if I ought to appoint a Vicar?"

"I am quite certain if you do, His Lordship will take an instant dislike to him!"

"You are probably right there," Gerry agreed, "so it would be a good idea to wait."

In a voice he could hardly hear, Olivia said:

"If he . . . turns us out of Green Gables for what I have . . . done in his . . . absence . . . where shall . . . I . . . go?"

"Throw you out?" Gerry asked. "I cannot believe he would dare do that! It is your nursing that has saved his life, and I will make certain that the Doctor tells him so."

"If he . . . stops Mama's money . . . we shall not be . . . able to stay here."

"As I have told you before, Olivia, you must save every penny of it, and actually, now that I have provided you with clothes, you should not have any expenses."

"Oh, Gerry, you have been wonderful, you know that!" Olivia said. "And having Mrs. Banks to cook our meals makes everything seem like a dream!"

It was Gerry who had suggested that while the Earl was staying at Green Gables, Mrs. Banks should cook for them there.

Mrs. Banks was only too delighted to oblige when he informed her she would be travelling in a carriage.

She drove from Chad to the village every morning, then back again in it at night.

"I feels like a Queen, Miss Olivia, I do really!" she said.

"If you do not mind working in our small kitchen," Olivia replied, "it will be wonderful to have you cooking us such fabulous food."

There was no necessity to tell Mrs. Banks how sparse their meals had been up until then.

Tony and Wendy never stopped saying so.

Even Gerry had to admit that he was putting on weight, and would soon need an elephant to carry him rather than a horse.

With Mrs. Banks in her carriage came a housemaid to help Bessie, as well as two footmen to carry trays upstairs and wait on them at mealtimes.

Occasionally Upton came, too, and the house seemed to be bursting at the seams with so many people in it.

But Olivia knew it was as happy as it had been when her Father and Mother were alive.

Everybody seemed to be laughing.

There was always some ridiculous story for Gerry to tell them.

It might be about what had happened at the Slate Mine or in one of the cottages which was being repaired.

Tony was more concerned with the horses than anything else.

He rode, Olivia thought, from dawn to dusk.

She had never known him to be in such high spirits.

Wendy had not been forgotten.

The Village Seamstress, when she had the right material, was a wonderful dressmaker.

She had made Wendy two very elegant dresses and was working on a third.

She looked so pretty in them that Olivia for the first time for a year asked some of their neighbours' children to tea.

Mrs. Banks cooked them delicious cakes, also gingerbread biscuits in the shape of little men and animals.

They enjoyed every mouthful.

Olivia was aware that the mothers of the children who came in answer to her invitation were naturally very curious.

By this time the whole of Oxfordshire was aware of what was happening at Chad.

When they gave a second, rather larger party at Chad, there was not a single refusal.

"We have been so looking forward to meeting the Earl," one of the Mothers said to Olivia, "and if he is as charming as Gerald, who, of course, we have known since he was a small boy, he will be welcomed with open arms."

The speaker went on to explain what they expected of him: that he would support the Hunt, be the Chairman of several Charities and, of course, race his horses.

The late Earl had started to do this several years before William and John were killed.

"It was such a pity that the last Earl gave up his racing-stable," a Lady said, "but I am sure we can persuade the new owner to race again."

"You must certainly try," Olivia replied.

Other visitors made searching questions about the Earl as a man.

Olivia suspected they thought she was trying to "set her cap" at the Earl or at Gerry.

It was then she remembered that the Earl had said she and Gerry had to marry each other.

She shivered at the thought that this was another problem which was waiting for them in the future.

She realised that Gerry had changed a great deal in the last weeks since he had assumed authority.

He had been hesitant at first and had asked her advice about everything.

But he had gradually taken the initiative himself.

She was aware he was, as her father would have said, "very much more of a man."

At the same time, there was no question of his being the man of her dreams.

When he was teasing Tony or fighting playfully with him, she thought they might have been the same age.

"Luncheon is served, Ma'am!" a footman said from the door.

Olivia walked to the Dining-Room, very conscious of her new gown.

As she and Gerry sat down, Tony and Wendy, who had been playing in the garden, came hurrying in to join them.

"What do you think, Olivia?" Tony said. "Gerry has had the fountain repaired!"

"Has it been done? How exciting!" Olivia exclaimed.

"I'se going to have goldfish in it!" Wendy said.

"You will have to be careful you do not fall into it," Gerry remarked, "or you might turn into a goldfish yourself!"

Wendy was delighted at the idea.

"Then she would have a tail and be able to swim much better than I can in the lake."

"Have you been swimming in the lake?" Gerry asked.

"We did when it was so hot in the Summer," Olivia admitted, "but it is too far to walk there in a bathing dress and difficult to change our clothes behind the bushes."

"That has given me an idea!" Gerry exclaimed. "We will have a large summer-house built on one side of the lake, where we can change, and I will order a boat to be built so that we can go upstream."

"That will be fun!" Wendy cried. "I'se wanted to go in a boat."

Olivia looked at Gerry in consternation.

She knew that somebody had only to suggest an idea and he immediately wanted to put it into operation.

"A summer-house and a boat are really not necessities!" she said.

"Nonsense!" Gerry replied. "The summer-house will be made by local labour and so will the boat, if anyone is capable of building it!"

"I hear there is a very good carpenter at Little Plowder," Tony said.

This was a village at the far end of the Chad Estate.

"Then I will certainly go to have a talk with him," Gerry replied.

Olivia wanted to expostulate, but she knew it would be useless.

She tried not to think of how angry the Earl would be when he found all these extra items had been ordered.

At the same time, she knew it was through Gerry that the whole village was now a different place.

Everybody looked happy and well fed.

They had certainly gorged themselves the first week.

She had gasped when she learnt how many oxen and sheep they had consumed.

Their large bills from the shops horrified her.

It was Mr. Bentick who had shown them to her, shaking his head and saying:

"I do not know what His Lordship is going to say, Miss Olivia!"

"That is what frightens me too!" Olivia said. "At the same time, he ought to be grateful that we saved the House from being burnt to the ground, and the villagers from rioting!"

They finished luncheon.

"Are you coming riding with us this afternoon?" Tony asked. "I want to show you some new jumps I have had erected on the flat ground beyond the paddock."

"Yes, of course I am," Olivia replied.

She ran upstairs to change from her new gown into a riding-habit which had also been included with Gerry's purchases.

'Mama used to say: "Make hay while the sun shines," ' she thought. 'That is what I am doing, and it is no use worrying about the cold winds and the snow which will come later.'

She changed quickly, knowing that the men disliked being kept waiting.

Then, as she came out of her own bed-room, she crossed the passage.

She went to see if the Earl was all right.

He was very still, but not as pale as he had been when he was just injured.

The Doctor had suggested that she gradually give him less and less of the herbs which made him sleep.

"He has to come back to reality sooner or later," Dr. Emmerson said.

"Yes . . . of course," Olivia had agreed in a small voice.

She stood looking down at the man in the bed.

He was now not the overbearing person he had been when she had first met him.

He was merely a handsome, ordinary man recovering from a wound he might have received in a war, though in fact he had been nearly killed by a youth who was suffering from hunger.

Supposing when he was better it happened all over again and the next time he did not recover?

And after that Chad went up in flames?

Then everybody who lived on the Estate would be hungry and weak, as they had been before.

Because the idea was so frightening, Olivia put her hand on the Earl's where it lay outside the sheet.

She thought it might be cold—the cold of death.

Instead, it was warm, the hand of a living man.

With a little murmur she turned away from the bed.

She ran down the stairs as if she were escaping not from the Earl, but from her own thoughts.

Outside in the sunshine Gerry and Tony were already mounted on the superb horses they had bought.

They were waiting for her impatiently.

A groom helped her into the side-saddle and they rode away, Wendy waving to them from the doorstep.

Mrs. Dawson was coming in a few minutes to take her out to tea with two of her nieces.

They had arrived unexpectedly to stay in her small house at the end of the village.

Wendy loved being with children of her own age.

Mrs. Banks had cooked a special cake for her to take as a present for Mrs. Dawson.

As Olivia rode under the oak trees in the Park she could see the spotted deer.

She was certain none of them had been touched since the youths were earning money and were no longer hungry.

'They are all happy now,' she thought. 'But when His Lordship wakes up, we may find this is just a dream!'

* * *

The Earl opened his eyes and wondered where he was.

Then he saw a small face not far from his own and thought he must be looking at an Angel.

It was a pink-and-white little face, with two large blue eyes over which the eye-lashes curved upwards.

The Angel had fair hair, and the sun shining through the windows turned it to a spun gold halo.

" 'Oos awake," a young voice said.

"Where—am I?" the Earl asked.

" 'Oos in Green Gables," the Angel answered, "and I'se wery, wery sorry for 'oo."

"Why—are you—sorry for—me?" the Earl asked.

It was difficult to speak except in jerks.

He thought he had heard the name Green Gables before, but he could not think where.

"I'se sorry for 'oo," the Angel went on, " 'cos 'Livia says nobody loves 'oo."

It seemed a strange statement.

Then vaguely the name " 'livia" meant something to him, although it did not seem quite right.

He shut his eyes.

"Are 'oo wery tired?" the Angel asked.

"I—think—so," the Earl answered. "Have I—been asleep for—long?"

"A long, long time!" the Angel replied.

It was all very puzzling, and his brain could not sort it out.

He shut his eyes again.

The Angel must have gone back to whatever Heaven she had come from.

* * *

The Earl was aware of very low voices.

"His Lordship's not stirred since I've been here!" a man's voice said.

The Earl recognised it was Higgins speaking.

He knew his voice only too well.

"You goes t'bed, Miss Olivia, and I'll stay on here."

"No, no, of course not. You have done so much all day, and you took my place to-night only because we had such an exciting dinner-party at Chad. It was such fun, and everybody said they had never enjoyed themselves so much."

"That's how it should be!" Higgins said. "But you go t'bed, 'cos I thinks 'Is Lordship be well enough now t'be left on his own."

"Very well, Higgins. I will go to bed if you will. If you leave the door open, I am sure you will hear if His Lordship is restless."

"I knows I will," Higgins said, "so orf you goes,

Miss, an' get your 'Beauty Sleep.' "

"You are . . . quite certain it is all right?"

"Sure as I'm standing 'ere!"

"Then . . . good-night, Higgins, and thank you very much for being so wonderful!"

The Earl heard the soft movements of Olivia leaving the room, then heavier footsteps as Higgins, too, left.

The Earl opened his eyes.

He knew now that it was Olivia Lambrick who was speaking to Higgins.

He was in Green Gables, the house where she lived.

It had been occupied by her Father, the Vicar, before he had died.

Then he remembered feeling furiously angry and something striking him.

There was an agony of pain in his chest and he had fallen backwards.

That was why he must have been carried here.

But—who was giving a party at Chad in his absence?

It seemed strange and impertinent on their part.

He was, however, too tired to try and puzzle it out.

He shut his eyes and went back into the darkness of sleep.

*   *   *

The Earl was aware that it was daytime.

There had been people tidying his bed and moving quietly about the room.

They obviously did not want to waken him, and he did not wish to be woken.

He thought it would be an effort to have to speak to anyone.

He did not yet feel well enough.

Then there was silence and he knew he was alone.

He tried to think, but there seemed no reason for him to do so.

He found himself remembering the Angel who had told him that nobody loved him.

Then, even as he thought about her, he was aware that once again she was beside him.

He opened his eyes.

She was looking even more angelic than she had before.

"I'se brought 'oo a rose."

She put it on the bed just in front of him, and he said:

"That was—very kind of—you!"

"I thought 'oo'd be pleased."

"I am—very—pleased!" the Earl assured her.

"Has no one ever given 'oo a rose before?"

"No one!"

"That is 'cos no one loves 'oo," Wendy said. "Would 'oo like me to love 'oo?"

Her eyes were very blue, as blue as a Summer sky.

There was a faint smile on the Earl's lips as he said:

"Yes—I would—like you to—love me."

"I will love 'oo," Wendy said, "and Emma will love 'oo too."

"Who is—Emma?" the Earl asked.

Wendy held up the doll she was holding in one hand.

It was a dilapidated doll, but she had been Wendy's favourite possession ever since she was tiny.

She had Emma beside her in bed; she took Emma with her wherever she went.

She talked to her as if she were a real person.

"So—that is—Emma!" the Earl said.

"Emma thinks it is wery sad no one loves 'oo."

The Earl did not speak, and after a moment Wendy said:

"Everyone loved my Dadda 'cos he loved me and all see people he looked after. I 'spects if 'oo looked after people they'd love 'oo too."

"I doubt it," the Earl remarked. "People are—very ungrateful!"

"I'se grateful," Wendy said.

"What for?" the Earl asked.

"For the gorgeous food I'se eating now Mrs. Banks comes to see us every day. I'se never a 'hole' in my tummy now!"

"Is that what—you had before—she came?" the Earl enquired.

Wendy nodded.

"When I'se had nothing to eat for supper, it would hurt me at night and I couldn't sleep."

"Why did—you not have—enough—food?" the Earl asked.

" 'Livia says it was 'cos we had no money. 'Oo cannot have food if 'oo cannot pay for it!"

"You must—have had—something!" the Earl said.

"On'y wabbits and lots of 'tatoes—not like the lovely things I'se eating now. We had salmon for luncheon—a great big salmon!"

She put her head on one side.

"It looked like see goldfish Cousin Gerry has put in the fountain, on'y much, much bigger!"

"Is your Cousin Gerald here?" the Earl asked.

"Yes," Wendy answered. "And he's got everyone in the village working and getting big, big wages. It makes 'livia wery, wery happy!"

There was silence. Then the Earl asked:

"What—else is he—doing?"

There was the sound of a door shutting somewhere downstairs.

Wendy slipped off the bed.

"I'se got to go," she said in a whisper. "I was told not to come in here, but I so wanted to tell 'oo that Emma and me loves 'oo."

"Thank you," the Earl said.

She had already gone, and he doubted if she heard him.

He wondered what was happening since he had been ill.

He had realised this morning that somebody was dressing a wound on his chest.

He had not opened his eyes because he did not want to know about it.

It was much easier to slip away into the darkness and not have to think.

Yet now his brain was working, and he thought over what Wendy had just said.

He realised who she was.

She was the child he had suggested should be placed in an Orphanage.

That would not happen if her sister married Gerald.

Perhaps they had already been married?

He thought it unlikely before he forced them to do so.

But—Gerald had got everybody working!

How could he have done that? And who was paying them for doing so?

The question seemed to be buzzing in his head.

"I do not—want to—know too—soon—I want to be—left—alone."

He was not certain whether he said the words aloud or merely thought them.

He was drifting away once again into a darkness where there were no problems.

chapter five

"GERRY is late!" Tony said.

"I expect he is riding and has forgotten the time," Olivia replied.

They both knew that Gerry rode early every morning to look at the Farms and the Slate Mine.

Then he arrived for breakfast with them.

"If there is anything I dislike," he said, "it is eating alone!"

Olivia was aware that if he could, he would have stayed with them at Green Gables.

But there was no room, and he had to stay at Chad whether he liked it or not.

She thought perhaps he was lonely in the Big House.

That was another thing the Earl would be when he had recovered from his injury.

It might set him even more against people than he was already.

He would be even more suspicious that they

were deceiving him in some way.

But it was no use thinking about that.

There was the sound of horse's hoofs outside, and the next minute Gerry burst into the room.

"What do you think?" he asked. "I have accepted for us all to go to a dinner-party to-night."

"A dinner-party?" Olivia exclaimed.

"Yes, and you will never guess who it is with!"

"I hope it is somebody exciting!" Tony said.

"Grand is the right word!" Gerry said. "And Upton is extremely impressed!"

They laughed and Olivia asked:

"Well? Who is it?"

"Lady Sheldon!" Gerry replied.

"She certainly is grand!" Tony agreed. "She never thought Papa was smart enough to be invited to any of the parties she gave."

"We are dining there to-night," Gerry said. "A groom arrived just when I was leaving and waited for an answer, so I said yes."

"I cannot go with you," Olivia said.

"Why not?" Gerry enquired. "I ordered an evening-gown for you!"

Olivia looked embarrassed.

The only dinner-party she had been to had been at Chad.

Four friends of Gerry's had turned up unexpectedly and stayed for dinner.

There was no question of their changing their clothes, so no one else wore evening-dress.

Now she said apologetically:

"Oh, Gerry, it is an awful thing to say, but I forgot about it! When I unpacked it I thought it was something I would never need."

"You will want several more if we are going to go to dinner-parties with people whom we will have to invite back."

Olivia looked at him in consternation.

"Do be careful! His Lordship is much better, but if he hears you are giving riotous parties at Chad, I am sure he will have a relapse!"

"Then we will not tell him," Gerry said simply, "but we will certainly dine with Lady Sheldon to-night."

Olivia knew it was considered a great honour to receive an invitation from the widow of the late Lord Chamberlain.

Lord Sheldon had been one of the outstanding personalities at the Court, first of King George III, then of his son, the present King.

He was respected and admired by everybody who knew him.

In Oxfordshire, where he had his county seat, he was spoken of in awe.

His wife came from one of the oldest families in England.

She had made it clear that she entertained only the people she considered important enough to be their personal friends.

The Duke and Duchess of Marlborough from Blenheim Palace were, of course, frequent guests, and just a few other distinguished neighbours.

The old Earl had always been welcome.

But his relations, much to the annoyance of some of them, were not on Lady Sheldon's list.

"I shall certainly look forward to seeing the house!" Tony said. "I wonder if I will be able to have a peep at the stables?"

"Oh, Tony, if we do go, you must behave yourself," Olivia said, "or we will never be asked again!"

Tony grinned.

"We are being asked now only because of Gerry. I do not mind betting Lady Sheldon thinks he may be the Seventh Earl and wants to entertain him before everyone else comes knocking on the door at Chad!"

"For whatever reason," Gerry said blithely, "I will pick you both up in the family barouche at seven o'clock."

Olivia was about to protest once again that she would stay at home.

Then she thought that just for once it would be very exciting to wear an evening-gown and go to a grand party.

It was doubtless something which would never occur again.

She knew her Mother would want her to go.

"We will be ready," she said to Gerry, "and I will tell Mrs. Banks she need not come back for dinner."

"She must certainly be here for luncheon," Gerry said, "and I am hungry now."

He rose as he spoke to help himself for the second time from a dish that was standing on the sideboard.

Tony did the same thing.

Olivia wondered how she would ever be able to feed them, if and when the Earl put a stop to their getting everything they ate from Chad.

Then, because it was something she did not want to think about, she said:

"I am coming riding with you both this morning, so I had better go and see if Bessie wants me to help her change the Earl's bandages."

She left the room and Gerry said to Tony:

"Is he really better?"

There was no doubt to whom he was referring, and Tony replied:

"Higgins says so, and the Doctor, who now comes only every other day unless we send for him, also thinks so."

Gerry heaved a deep sigh.

"I shall miss being the Boss once Lenox is back!"

"You have been magnificent!" Tony exclaimed. "No one else would have succeeded in doing all the things you have done!"

"I expect I shall pay for it!" Gerry said ruefully.

"It will be unfair if you do!" Tony replied.

"It is strange," Gerry ruminated, "but I have only just realised how much I enjoy the country, and having been brought up in it how much I know about farming."

"The Farmers are all delighted with you!" Tony remarked. "I have never known Hampton, who is a dour man, be so enthusiastic about anybody!"

"I used to think, when I was in London," Gerry went on as if he were thinking it out for himself, "that nothing could be more exciting than going to gaming Clubs, chatting to the 'Cyprians' in the White House, or attending riotous evenings at the Coal Hole."

"I have not had a chance to go to any of them!" Tony said.

"I expect you will, sooner or later," Gerry replied, "but I can tell you, there is nothing more exciting than riding good horses, seeing the crops growing, the sheep lambing, and the cows giving enough milk, simply because you have given the right orders."

Tony looked at him in surprise before he asked: "What will you do when you leave here?"

"I have not the slightest idea," Gerry replied. "I only know that London will seem disappointing and the tinsel will no longer glitter enticingly."

Before he could say any more, the door opened and Olivia came in.

"Everything is under control," she said. "Bessie does not need my help, and Miss Dawson has arrived to look after Wendy. Now all I want to do is to ride as far and as quickly as we can and think about nothing else."

"That is just what I want to do," Gerry said, "and the horses are waiting for us by now."

It was so like him, Olivia thought, to have ordered Graves before he left Chad to bring her a horse with a side-saddle.

She gave him a grateful smile, and he smiled back.

When they went outside, he lifted her onto the saddle.

"Thank goodness you ride well!" he exclaimed. "I cannot stand a woman who is heavy in the saddle and cow-fisted with the reins!"

Olivia laughed and rode ahead of the two men into the Park.

* * *

"Now, don't you dare let His Lordship move an' open up his wound!" Bessie said to Higgins. "It be a miracle it's healed the way it had, and it'd break me heart to start all over again!"

"He's not moved the last three nights," Higgins replied.

"It's only due to you an' Miss Olivia," Bessie said, "that when 'e was wild with fever he didn't tear hisself to pieces!"

"It were Miss Olivia, not me!" Higgins retorted. "'Er puts her arms round him, cradles his head against her, and soothes his forehead as if he were a child!"

"What we'd do without her, I don't know!" Bessie said. "They talks about her in the village as if her were a Saint. It wouldn't surprise me if they puts up a statue to her!"

"It'd be no more than she deserves!" Higgins agreed. "I hears it were her as told Mr. Gerald wot to do."

"'Course it were!" Bessie replied. "Who else would have thought of opening the Slate Mine or repairing the Vicarage? A real nice house that's going to be!"

"Then they'd better get a real nice man to put in it!" Higgins remarked.

Bessie sighed.

"There'll never be another one like the Reverend! If ever a man come straight from God t'was he! This house were a little bit of Heaven, 'til His Lordship died and then it was like Hell."

"Has it really bin as bad as that?" Higgins asked.

"Worse!" Bessie said. "Us was so hungry, if it hadn't bin for the rabbits, we'd be in our graves by now!"

"Then let's hope it don't happen again!"

As Higgins spoke doubtfully, he looked at his master.

"If it does, Mr. Higgins," Bessie said brusquely, "I can tell you I'll strangle His Lordship with me own hands!"

"Go on with you!" Higgins said. "You'd never do a thing like that!"

"Don't you be too sure!" Bessie said ominously.

She pulled the Earl's nightshirt over his naked chest and buttoned it down the front.

Then she said to him in the tone of a strict but affectionate Nanny:

"Now, you be a good boy an' don't go upsetting my handiwork!"

"Do you think he can hear you?" Higgins asked.

"If he can, he'll do as he's told!" Bessie answered.

She picked up the cardboard box containing the dressings and walked towards the door.

"There's a nice cup o' tea waitin' for you downstairs, Mr. Higgins."

"Then I'll come and have it!" Higgins replied.

He followed her down the stairs, and the Earl could hear them laughing as they went.

He opened his eyes and thought he felt better to-day.

In fact, he had been going to speak to Higgins.

Then Bessie had come into the room, and he felt it was too much of an effort to talk to both of them.

Their conversation, however, had been enlightening.

So it was Olivia who had been able to send him to sleep when he was burning with a fever which had seemed to set his whole body on fire.

When he thought it over carefully, he realised that the drink she gave him also had something to do with it.

He had been aware that for the last two or three days he was being fed every three hours with something he drank.

There were two things. The first tasted like a delicious soup.

Yesterday he had heard Higgins whisper to Gerry that its ingredients were the best beef, a hare, and a young lamb.

The other drink was one that had been sweetened with honey.

He had heard Olivia say to him as she raised his head:

"Now it is time for your healing herbs, and you must be very good and swallow it all."

She had no idea that he was listening to her.

But when he looked back into the darkness he realised that she talked to him every time she fed him.

She talked to him even when the fever made him toss from side to side.

When she was close he was aware of the scent of lavender.

"I am better!" he told himself now. "When Higgins comes back, I will ask for something to eat. The sooner I am up and see what is happening, the better!"

These were brave words.

At the same time, he knew he dreaded coming back to a world which was strange, a world in which things had been happening he did not understand.

It would be a great effort to come back.

It was much easier to slip away into the darkness where there were no problems.

Then he heard a little voice beside him say:

"Is 'oo weally asleep, or only 'tending?"

He opened his eyes to find Wendy beside him, holding Emma in her arms.

For the first time, she was wearing a bonnet which framed her small face and the front of her fair hair.

"Are—you going—out?" the Earl asked.

"I'se going to have luncheon with two little girls like me," Wendy replied, "and Emma's going too, so I'se come to say good-bye to 'oo."

"I hope—you have—a nice—time," the Earl said.

"It'll be fun, and Mrs. Banks has baked a lovely cake for us."

The Earl smiled.

Wendy put her hand on top of his.

"Bessie says that when 'oo's well Mrs. Banks'll go back to the Big House and we'll have nothing to eat."

"That—is not—true," the Earl said firmly.

"I'll not have a big hole in my tummy again?"

There was an anxious expression in the blue eyes.

"I—promise—that will—not happen," the Earl said.

Wendy's whole face lit up as if there were a light inside her.

" 'Oo promise? 'Oo really promise?"

"I—promise!" he said.

She bent forward and kissed him on the cheek.

"Thank 'oo, thank 'oo! And Emma thanks 'oo too!"

She glanced towards the door.

"I must go," she said, " 'cos if Bessie finds me here, she'll be angry and tell 'livia."

"Then—hurry," the Earl said, "but come—and see me—again soon."

"I will," Wendy answered.

She walked out the door and the Earl heard her running down the stairs.

He thought with a little twist of his lips that he had given her a promise which he would have to keep.

Then, because he did not want to think about the future, he shut his eyes and tried to sleep.

*   *   *

Olivia took a last glance at herself in the mirror and knew she had never looked so pretty.

The gown Gerry had ordered for her was white.

There were small bunches of snowdrops around the hem and the same flowers tucked under the puffed sleeves.

It was the first time she had worn an evening-gown cut so low in the bodice.

She hoped it was not immodest.

When she went downstairs, Tony surprisingly told her she looked lovely.

"You look very smart yourself!" she replied. "And do not forget that we have to represent the family, who have never before been invited to Lady Sheldon's house."

"I call it rather exciting," Tony said, "and I am sure you are right in thinking that she is counting on Gerry becoming the next Earl."

"She will be disappointed," Olivia answered.

"Bessie says the Earl's wound is practically healed, and he is looking almost himself again."

Gerry held up his hands in horror.

"That is exactly what I am afraid of!" he exclaimed.

Olivia could not help laughing.

* * *

They arrived at Sheldon Hall, which was even larger than Chad, but not so beautiful.

It was impossible, however, not to be impressed by the red carpet up which they walked into a hall where there were more footmen than Olivia had ever seen before.

The Drawing-Room was enormous with three crystal chandeliers ablaze with candles.

Lady Sheldon was wearing a large tiara which glittered in their light.

There were thirty people to dinner.

Olivia was grateful to Gerry when she realised that she could hold her own with the most elegantly gowned women she had ever seen.

She had been told that the party was being given for Lady Sheldon's granddaughter, Lucinda, who was the same age as herself.

She was very pretty with dark hair and flashing eyes.

She was seated next to Gerry, who obviously found her fascinating.

After dinner a number of other young people arrived, who had been dining in neighbouring houses.

There was an Orchestra in another room which was as large as the Drawing-Room.

It was a long time since Olivia had danced.

She was nervous in case she should be clumsy and stumble over her partners' feet.

The man she was dancing with said:

"I find you entrancing! Why have I not seen you before?"

"I live here in the country," Olivia replied.

"Then that accounts for it," he answered. "If you had attended any Ball in London, it would be impossible for me to forget you!"

She thought he was only being flattering and laughed.

"It is true," he said, "and I assure you, having found you, I shall not lose you again!"

He certainly made himself very attentive.

She found herself dancing with him so many times that she felt sure she was doing something which was incorrect.

"Mama told me," she said, "that it was wrong to dance with the same man too often, although it is very kind of you to ask me."

"That may be true at a London Ball," he replied, "but here we can enjoy ourselves, and as I am staying in the house, I must obviously look after my hostess's guests."

"There are quite a number of other guests besides me," Olivia pointed out.

"But none of them so lovely, nor do I find them irresistible, as I find you!"

The way he spoke made her feel shy.

She looked round for Gerry or Tony.

Gerry was dancing with their hostess's grand-daughter.

She had the idea it was the third or fourth time he had done so.

Tony had disappeared.

She hoped he had not slipped away to the stables.

"You are looking worried," her partner said, "and that I cannot allow!"

"I was wondering what had happened to my brother."

"I feel sure he can look after himself, so just think of me."

Olivia smiled.

"I can hardly do that when I do not even know your name!"

"It is Mortimer Holden and, to be formal, I am a Baronet, but that is something I do not want you to be."

"How can I be anything else when I have only just met you?"

"I have only just met you," he replied, "and I know already that I want to know you better—in fact I am afraid to say how much."

Olivia felt shy.

She also thought he was somewhat overpowering.

She was sensible enough to refuse to go into the Conservatory when he asked her to do so.

She insisted they must remain in the room in which they were dancing.

When Gerry came to ask her for a dance, she felt relieved.

"You are making yourself rather conspicuous with Holden!" he remarked.

"I know," Olivia replied, "but he keeps asking me to dance, and it is difficult for me to say no."

"He is not a chap I care for," Gerry said. "But he goes everywhere, and fancies himself as a 'ladies' man!' "

"What do you mean by that?" Olivia asked innocently.

"I mean that he runs after every pretty woman who takes his fancy and, if she takes him at all seriously, he is off like a shot, looking for another!"

"He sounds horrid!" Olivia said. "I do not want to dance with him again."

"Then I will take care that you do not!" Gerry replied.

When their dance ended, he introduced a young man in the party who asked her to dance.

He produced others, and she did not dance again with Sir Mortimer Holden.

When they drove home Olivia said:

"It was a lovely party, and thank you, Gerry, for all those men to whom you introduced me. Most of them wanted to talk about horses, so I found that easy!"

"Do you know what Lady Sheldon said to me?" Gerry asked.

"I saw her talking to you very earnestly at dinner!" Tony remarked.

"She said she had been hearing of the success of everything I have done at Chad," Gerry went on, "and she was very impressed that I had re-opened the Slate Mine. She said there is one on her Estate and asked me if I would go over to-morrow and advise her whether it would be a viable proposition to open it again."

"Good gracious!" Tony exclaimed. "Will you be able to give her the right answer?"

"I hope so," Gerry replied. "But I will ask Cutler for a few hints first!"

"If you are not careful," Olivia teased, "Chad will lose you and you will be revolutionising Sheldon!"

Gerry did not answer for a moment. Then he said:

"That is the sort of thing that happens only in books!"

He was silent for a while. Then Olivia asked:

"I thought Lucinda, Lady Sheldon's granddaughter, was very pretty, and you must have thought the same!"

There was a little pause before Gerry said:

"I did, and she is also extremely intelligent."

Olivia wanted to ask him what they had talked about.

Then she thought he might think she was prying, and lapsed into silence.

She thought perhaps Gerry was tired, and on the other side of her, Tony had fallen asleep.

"It was an evening I shall never forget," she told herself, "and perhaps I shall never know another one like it."

*   *   *

The Earl was woken by the sound of a thunderstorm.

It was some distance away, and he thought it was like the roar of cannons during a battle.

The next clap of thunder was nearer, and as he listened to it, the door opened and Wendy came in to the room.

"Emma's . . . frightened!" she said with a little tremor in her voice.

"Then you were right to bring her to me," the Earl said.

Wendy reached the bed and, climbing up onto it, wriggled between the sheets and blankets to move close to the Earl.

For a moment he was surprised, then his arm went round her and she said:

"Now it is . . . like being . . . with Dadda."

As she spoke, there was another clap of thunder almost overhead, and she hid her face on his shoulder.

He could feel her small body trembling against his, and instinctively his arm tightened.

"It is all right," he said gently. "It is just the clouds banging into each other because they are so clumsy."

"I'se not . . . frightened," Wendy said, "but Emma does not . . . like the . . . noise!"

"It will go away soon."

"I am safe . . . here with . . . 'oo, and Dadda used to . . . tell me a . . . story."

"I do not know any stories," the Earl replied, "so perhaps you had better tell me one."

" 'oo do not . . . know any . . . stories?" Wendy asked.

"Not the ones you have been told."

Wendy thought for a moment. Then she said:

"I like stories where people live happily ever after, and there is no Ogre to gobble them up, or make them frightened."

"Then you tell me a story like that," the Earl said.

"I thought about 'oo last night," Wendy said. "I thought 'oo were like the Knight in Shining Armour

111

that Olivia tells me about."

"What does the Knight do?"

"He is wery, wery brave," Wendy explained. "He fought a big Ogre who was frightening everybody and making them cry. When the Ogre ran away, everyone was happy. They danced and had delicious cakes to eat."

"Is that what you expect me to do?" the Earl asked.

"It is what 'oo will do if 'oo are a Knight," Wendy said. "Knights are good and everyone loves them. Ogres are bad!"

There was another clap of thunder, and quickly she hid her face again.

"The storm is moving farther away," the Earl said. "The next time we hear it it will be quieter, then it will be quieter and quieter still until we cannot hear it any more."

"Emma's wery . . . glad 'oo is here," Wendy said in a sleepy voice, "and . . . now we are . . . safe . . . we can . . . go . . . to . . . sleep . . ."

Her voice trailed away.

The Earl realised to his surprise that was what had happened.

The child had fallen asleep in his arms.

It gave him a strange feeling that he never experienced before.

He wanted to protect her, to look after her.

He remembered he had already promised she should never "have a hole" in her tummy again.

*　　*　　*

The carriage stopped outside Green Gables and Tony woke up with a start.

112

"I have been asleep!" he murmured.

"It is nearly four o'clock in the morning," Gerry replied, "so it is not surprising."

"We need not hurry to-morrow," Olivia said. "I will leave a note for Bessie to tell her that breakfast will be later."

Gerry smiled.

"I will try not to be late, but if I am, keep something hot for me."

"Mrs. Banks will see to that," Olivia said. "You know you are her favourite. When she tells me what we are having for luncheon or dinner she always says:

'It's wot Mr. Gerald likes, an' I want to please him!' "

Olivia mimicked Mrs. Banks's voice and Gerry said:

"If you are jealous of Mrs. Banks being in your house, I shall take her back to Chad and keep her all to myself!"

"Now you are undoubtedly bullying me," Olivia replied, "and I shall retire with dignity!"

Gerry helped her out of the carriage.

Before she went into the house, she kissed his cheek.

"Thank you for a lovely, lovely evening," she said. "I enjoyed it all and we would never have been asked but for you!"

"We will have a dance at Chad and ask Lucinda to it," Gerry answered.

Olivia went into the hall and Tony, yawning loudly, followed her.

"I am dead on my feet!" he said.

"But I am sure you will not be too tired to ride

to-morrow!" Olivia smiled.

"Of course not!" he answered.

He dragged himself up the stairs, and she knew that after a long day's riding, and dancing for hours, he was exhausted.

She was feeling rather tired herself.

She blew out the candles which Higgins had left burning in the hall.

She was just about to go to her own bed-room.

Then she thought she should peep in at the Earl and see if he was all right.

She saw that Higgins's door was ajar, and he would have heard him if he had called.

At the same time, she should reassure herself that he was sleeping peacefully.

She opened the door.

She was surprised to see there was one candle alight by the bed.

It seemed strange that Higgins had not blown it out.

She naturally had no idea that Higgins had looked in at his Master before he retired.

To his astonishment, the Earl was lying with his eyes open.

He had put his fingers to his lips and waved a hand to tell him to go away.

'I will blow out the candle,' Olivia thought. 'It could be dangerous to leave it burning.'

She moved nearer to the bed, then stopped still.

The Earl's head was resting on the white linen-covered pillow, but he was not alone.

His eyes were closed and he was obviously asleep, as was Wendy, who was snuggled up close to him with Emma in her arms.

Olivia could only stare at them in astonishment. She blew out the candle.

Then she tip-toed out of the room, shutting the door very quietly behind her.

chapter six

OLIVIA awoke because Bessie came into her room carrying a tray.

She laid it down by the bed and pulled back the curtains.

"You have brought my breakfast up!" Olivia exclaimed. "It is very kind of you."

"As it happens, it's your lunch!" Bessie replied.

"My luncheon?" Olivia exclaimed.

"It's after half-past-twelve, Miss Olivia, and you've been sleeping like the dead!"

Olivia pushed her hair back from her eyes and said:

"I have never done such a thing before!"

"You've never been so late!" Bessie said. "Nearly four o'clock in the morning, before you gets to bed, Mr. Tony tells me. I've never heard such goings-on!"

She was, however, smiling.

Olivia knew she was in reality pleased that

they had enjoyed themselves.

"Where is everybody?" Olivia asked.

She took the cover off her plate as she spoke and found a delicious piece of fish covered with cream sauce.

Bessie was tidying the room.

"Mr. Gerald ate a big breakfast and went off to Sheldon Hall. Very posh we're getting these days!"

"They were impressed that he had opened the Slate Mine," Olivia said.

"And Mr. Tony's gone to Woodstock," Bessie went on, "because he heard last night there were some horses for sale which he's sure Mr. Gerald'll want to buy."

Olivia stopped eating and looked at Bessie with worried eyes.

The Earl was better.

She was wondering what he would say when he found his stables packed with well-bred but expensive horses.

"Wendy's in the kitchen," Bessie finished, "helping Mrs. Banks cook."

Olivia smiled.

She remembered how she had enjoyed learning to cook with her Mother when she had been the same age.

It had only palled when she had to cook every day and there was nothing to put in the pot but rabbit.

"Now, you just take it easy," Bessie admonished, "and there's no hurry for you to come fussing downstairs. With a maid from the Big House to help me, the place's as clean as a new pin!"

"You have always kept it like that," Olivia said.

She knew Bessie was pleased at the compliment, and she went from the room, saying:

"I only says to myself long may it last!"

Olivia was thinking the same thing.

Then she remembered how amazing it had been last night to see Wendy sleeping beside the Earl.

She had not realised there had been a thunderstorm while she was at Sheldon Hall.

She thought, however, she might have guessed it when the roads were so wet on the way home that the horses had to go slowly.

When she finished her luncheon she got up and dressed slowly.

She was thinking how nice it was for once to have nothing to do.

The housemaid from Chad and Bessie had watered the flowers, which was something she always did herself.

When she got downstairs she went into the Sitting-Room to look out through the open windows onto the garden.

It was a long time since she had been able just to think instead of actively do something.

The Earl would be resting now.

A little later she would take some flowers to his bed-room.

She had arranged flowers in his room every day, even while he had been unconscious.

Her Mother had always said she thought a room looked empty without flowers.

'I will take him roses or perhaps lilies if there are any out,' she decided.

The door behind her opened, and thinking it was Bessie, she said:

"The garden is looking lovely, and having a gardener from Chad makes all the difference!"

Bessie did not answer, and Olivia turned her head.

Then she started.

It was not Bessie she was seeing, but Sir Mortimer Holden.

"The front-door was open, so I came in," he explained.

"I . . . I was not . . . expecting . . . you!" Olivia stammered.

He smiled.

"You must have known last night that I had no intention of letting you escape from me so easily."

He came to stand beside her at the window.

"I wanted to see you again," he said, "to find out if you were as beautiful in the daytime as you were last night—and the answer is yes. You are, if possible, even lovelier!"

Olivia took a step away from him.

"Y-you are . . . embarrassing me," she said shyly. "Can I offer you any . . . refreshment?"

"All I want to do is to talk to you," Sir Mortimer replied.

Olivia said nothing, and he went on:

"I have learnt from my hostess that your Father was the Vicar, but you are quite unlike any Vicar's daughter I have ever seen before!"

"Perhaps you have not seen very many," Olivia said, trying to move farther away from him.

"I have certainly never seen one who looks like you," he said, "and who makes me feel I want to wrap her in sables and decorate her with diamonds!"

There was something in the way he spoke which made Olivia feel uncomfortable.

"I am afraid that . . . neither Gerald nor . . . Tony are here at . . . the moment . . ." Olivia began.

"I want you to listen to me," Sir Mortimer said, "and stop trying to be evasive."

Olivia did not move, but she did not look at him and he went on:

"Lady Sheldon told me how poor you are, so I therefore suggest that I take you to London and give you all the things you have never had before, and I will teach you about love, which will be very exciting for me!"

Olivia looked at him in astonishment.

"I do not . . . know what . . . you are . . . saying, but I am sure it is . . . something you . . . should not . . . say to me!"

"Why should I waste words?" Sir Mortimer said.

With that he stepped forward, and before she realised what he was about to do, put his arms around her.

"I want to kiss you," he said in a thick voice, "more than I have ever wanted anything in my whole life!"

It was then Olivia realised what was happening.

"No! No!" she cried, struggling frantically against him.

She realised as she did so how very strong his arms were.

His lips were coming nearer and nearer to hers.

"Let me . . . go!" she cried. "You are . . . not to . . . touch me!"

"But I am touching you!" he said.

There was a gloating note in his voice, and the

expression in his eyes terrorised her.

She turned her head from side to side to avoid his lips.

Her cheek brushed his mouth, and she knew that he was repulsive.

"You are mine!" he said, and it seemed to her like the menacing growl of an animal. "Mine—and you cannot escape from me!"

She made one last frantic effort to do so.

Then, as she felt his mouth sear her cheek, she screamed.

As she did so, the door opened and Bessie said:

"Now, what's goin' on here, I'd like to know!"

Sir Mortimer's arms slackened.

With a strength Olivia did not know she possessed, she pushed him away.

She ran across the room past Bessie in the doorway and up the stairs.

Without really thinking, she opened the Earl's bed-room door and went inside.

Shutting it behind her, she leant against it limply.

For a moment she was completely breathless.

Then, as she just stood there, frightened that Sir Mortimer might pursue her, the Earl asked:

"What has happened? What has upset you?"

She looked towards the bed.

To her astonishment, she realised that he was not there but sitting in an arm-chair in the window.

He was not dressed, but was wearing a dark robe and his knees were covered with a blanket.

Without thinking, she ran towards him.

Because there seemed to be no chair available, she went down on her knees beside him.

She was still fighting for breath, still feeling her heart pounding tumultuously in her breast.

"What has upset you?" the Earl asked again.

"It was a . . . a man . . . a man I . . . met last . . . night."

The words were hardly audible.

She bent her head so that all he could see was the shining gold of her hair.

"I suppose he tried to kiss you!" the Earl said. "Why did you ask him here?"

"I . . . I did not . . . ask him!" Olivia replied indignantly. "H-he . . . just came!"

She took several breaths before she added:

"How . . . could I have . . . guessed that . . . a man I had . . . met only . . . once would . . . behave like that . . . or say . . . such . . . things to me!"

"Did he kiss you?" the Earl asked.

"Bessie . . . came into . . . the room . . . and saved me . . . but I was . . . frightened . . . very frightened!"

"And you came to me to save you."

Olivia just nodded.

Then with an effort to speak in an ordinary manner she said:

"I . . . I suppose . . . that is . . . what . . . Wendy did . . . last night."

"You are being as sensible as she was," the Earl said.

Olivia sat back on her heels.

"Perhaps I was . . . foolish to be . . . so frightened," she said, "but he is . . . a . . . horrible . . . loathsome man . . . and I could . . . not let him . . . kiss me."

"Have you never been kissed?" the Earl asked.

"No . . . of course . . . not!"

There was silence before the Earl said:

"I should have thought Gerald would have done so by now!"

Olivia was still.

"Gerry is . . . like my . . . brother," she said after a moment.

"But I understand you have been helping him."

Olivia dropped her head again.

Then she said in a very small voice:

"I hope . . . you will . . . understand . . . when you see . . . what has been done . . . and that everybody is very . . . very happy."

"That is what Wendy has been telling me," the Earl said surprisingly.

Olivia looked up at him, wondering what she should say.

Then the door opened.

"Miss Wendy wants to see Your Lordship," Higgins announced.

Wendy came very slowly through the door.

She was holding something in both her hands, and as she came across the room Olivia moved out of her way.

She was, however, still sitting on the floor, but not so close to the Earl.

Wendy was looking only at what she held in her hands.

It was a plate and on it, Olivia could see, there was a cake.

She reached the Earl.

"I'se a present for 'oo," she said, "an' I made it all by myself, but Mrs. Banks helped me a little bit."

"Just for me?" the Earl asked. "That is very kind of you!"

"Look at it!" Wendy said excitedly. "Look at what I'se written on it!"

The Earl took the plate from her.

Wendy leaned against his chair, her eyes shining.

The cake was a small one, covered with white icing, and written on it in pink were the words:

"I LOVE YOU"

"Thank you very much," the Earl said, "and you made this all yourself?"

"Mrs. Banks held my hand for the writing," Wendy said, "but it was me who wrote it."

"Of course it was," the Earl agreed, "and it is the nicest and prettiest cake I have ever seen!"

"Do 'oo really think that? Really truly?"

"Really truly!" he said solemnly.

Olivia was watching the two of them with astonishment.

Then, as she realised the Earl had nowhere to put the cake, she rose to her feet, saying:

"Shall I put it down for you until you have your tea?"

"Thank you."

She took the cake from him and put it on a table which was a little way across the room.

When she turned round she saw to her surprise that Wendy was sitting on the Earl's knee.

"It took me a long time to make 'oos cake," she said, "and Mrs. Banks has made some gingerbread people for tea, and 'oo must have one of those too."

"Of course I will," the Earl said, "but I will eat your cake first."

" 'oo can give Olivia a piece," Wendy said, "but not Tony 'cause he's greedy and he'll gobble it all up."

"I will not let him do that!" the Earl agreed. "And now, as you have given me a present, I must give you one."

"A present? All to myself?" Wendy asked.

"All to yourself," the Earl repeated. "Tell me something you really want."

Wendy thought for a moment. Then she said:

"I want something wery, wery much, but perhaps 'oo'll think it too big a present."

"Tell me what you want," the Earl said, "then I can decide if I can afford it."

Wendy looked at her sister.

" 'Livia'll say I'se greedy."

"Then suppose you whisper it in my ear so that Olivia will not hear?" the Earl suggested.

Wendy put her mouth close against his ear.

She spoke in what she thought was a whisper, but Olivia heard her say quite clearly:

"I want a pony all of my own!"

There was a little pause. Then the Earl said:

"As soon as I am well enough, we will go and find one together."

Wendy was looking at him.

She gave a cry, and in a voice that was like the song of a bird, she said:

" 'oo'll give me a pony, a real pony, just for me?"

"Just for you!" the Earl promised.

Then her arms were round his neck and she was

126

kissing his cheek not once, but a dozen times.

The Earl looked across the room at Olivia.

Seeing the astonishment on her face, he smiled.

* * *

Olivia was downstairs, waiting for Gerry.

It was already ten minutes past the usual time they had dinner.

He had not come in at tea-time and she supposed he was still at Sheldon Hall.

She wondered if perhaps he was staying there for dinner.

There was also no sign of Tony.

She suspected that whoever he had seen in Woodstock had persuaded him to stay on.

He would doubtless return very late.

She knew only too well that when men were talking about horses, they invariably forgot the time.

She was beginning however to think that Mrs. Banks's dinner would be spoilt.

Then she heard the footman who was to wait on them at dinner cross the hall and knew Gerry must have arrived.

He came in.

He had changed into his evening-clothes and was looking as smart as he had last night.

"I had given you up for lost!" she exclaimed as he walked towards her.

"You must forgive me," Gerry said, "and perhaps I should have let you know before, but I am dining at Sheldon Hall."

"But you have been there all day!" Olivia exclaimed.

"I know," he answered, "but there is a great

deal more to be discussed, so I just rushed home, had a bath, and changed. They are having dinner late so that I can join them. You do understand?"

"Of course I do," Olivia said. "The person who will be most disappointed is Mrs. Banks."

"Make my apologies," Gerry said, "and tell her I will eat double what I usually do to-morrow!"

He glanced at the clock and said:

"I must go. You will be all right?"

"Yes . . . of course," Olivia said.

He was gone.

She heard the horses driving away before she could reach the hall.

Feeling a little lost and forlorn, she waited for the footman to announce dinner.

She knew the news that Gerry was dining out would have already reached Mrs. Banks.

She felt disappointed, like a child who has been deprived of a promised treat.

The door opened.

She was about to rise to her feet to go into the Dining-Room, when she saw it was not the footman, but Higgins.

" 'Scuse me, Miss, but His Lordship asks that if Mr. Gerald ain't here for dinner, if you'll honour him by having dinner upstairs with him!"

Olivia stared at Higgins in astonishment.

"You are sure it will not be too much for him?" she asked.

"He's had a good rest, and a sleep, after tea," Higgins replied, "and I don't thinks as how it'd do him any harm."

"No . . . I suppose . . . not," Olivia said.

Then she could not help laughing.

It seemed so ridiculous that the Earl should be inviting her to dinner in his bed-room.

"It be all right, Miss," Higgins said. "I'll just get everything ready and help His Lordship outa bed."

He shut the door, and Olivia walked across the room to the window.

The curtains were not yet drawn and the sun was sinking behind the trees.

She could hear the rooks going to roost, but otherwise everything was quiet and still.

It made her feel as if something were going to happen.

She had no idea what it might be.

She only knew she was glad she was dining with the Earl.

She hated to be alone in the Dining-Room.

Before everything had changed, she would have eaten a scrap of something in the kitchen.

Anyway, there was never enough food for dinner as well as luncheon.

But now that Mrs. Banks was there to cook and a footman to wait on them, everything was different.

"How can we ever go . . . back to . . . what it was . . . before?" she asked.

Then, instead of the cloud of depression that usually swept over her when she thought of the future, there was a ray of hope.

In fact, it was bigger than a ray.

It was more like a star shining in the darkness of the sky.

"How," her logical brain asked her, "could the

Earl condemn them to penury and at the same time give Wendy a pony?"

The child had talked of nothing else since he had promised that was what he would do.

When Olivia had kissed her good-night, Wendy had said as she hugged her:

"I'se thinking of a name for my pony. A wery, wery special one, and I'll love him wery much, but I'll always love Emma the best!"

"Of course you will," Olivia said. "And you will be able to give Emma a ride on your pony."

It was as if Wendy were trying to solve the problem of Emma having her "nose put out of joint."

'And a pony will need a stable and a groom,' Olivia thought now, 'so he . . . may let us . . . stay on at . . . Green Gables.'

"Dinner is served, Miss!" the footman announced.

Olivia jumped up and walked eagerly up the stairs to the Earl's bed-room.

He was seated in the same chair he had been in during the afternoon.

Now, however, there was a small table in front of him and a chair for her.

Higgins had brought up the candles from the Dining-Room, also a candelabrum which lit up the whole room.

As Olivia sat down opposite the Earl, she realised he was wearing his dressing-gown and had a blanket over his knees.

There was a silk scarf round his neck.

It gave him, she thought, a somewhat raffish appearance, as if he were a pirate.

Then she smiled at her own thoughts.

The last thing she could imagine the Earl doing

was roaming the high seas and preying on other ships.

"Thank you for asking me to dine with you," she said. "I was just thinking that everybody had . . . forsaken me."

She spoke lightly, and the Earl replied:

"I thought that was what you might be feeling, and I have no wish to eat alone."

"But you must not do too much too quickly!" Olivia said automatically.

"Stop!" the Earl exclaimed. "Higgins has been preaching at me all day!"

"Then I will try not to do so," Olivia answered. "At the same time, you must be aware that we have been very worried about you."

"I know you saved my life," he said, "so you must have considered it was worth saving!"

Olivia looked at him in surprise.

"Who told you I saved your life?"

"Everyone who has come into this room!" the Earl replied. "And not once, but a thousand times!"

Olivia laughed.

"You should not believe all you hear, and you have been a very good patient. Bessie is very proud of you."

"So she has told me, not once, but a thousand times!"

They both laughed.

Then, as the footman poured some wine into her glass, Olivia exclaimed:

"Champagne? Are we celebrating something?"

"But of course!" the Earl answered. "We are celebrating the fact that I am alive and you are dining with me!"

"Then I must propose a toast!" Olivia said as she smiled.

She lifted her glass and tried to think what she should say.

Then, as she realised the Earl was waiting, she said:

"I wish you every happiness to-day, to-morrow, and for the rest of your life!"

It was the first toast she could remember, and she suspected she had heard it at a wedding.

"Thank you," the Earl said, "and I will let you know if your wish comes true."

Two footmen brought in the dishes Mrs. Banks had cooked for them.

The Earl managed to eat quite a lot which Olivia knew would please Bessie.

Only when they had finished and the footman and Higgins withdrew from the room did Olivia say:

"You must be tired, and Higgins will be angry with me if I keep you up late!"

"I am a little tired," the Earl admitted, "but I have enjoyed our dinner enormously, and I hope I shall soon be able to come downstairs. In fact, it is what I intend to do, if possible, to-morrow."

"It is too soon!" Olivia protested. "Much, much too soon!"

"I thought," the Earl went on as if she had not spoken, "we might drive round the village and the Estate so that you can show me some of the things you and Gerald have done while I have been unconscious."

Olivia drew in her breath.

They had been chatting so easily over dinner.

She had for the moment forgotten that now that the Earl was better, he would have to learn the truth.

After a moment, in a nervous little voice, she said:

"I suppose . . . you have . . . been told . . . some changes have . . . been . . . made?"

"You could hardly expect to keep it a secret from me," the Earl remarked.

"We had no . . . intention of . . . doing that," Olivia said, "but decisions . . . had to be . . . made, and Gerald has . . . been wonderful . . . absolutely wonderful!"

"And of course that is what I want to see, hear, and—understand."

There was just a pause before the last word, and Olivia bent forward.

"Will you . . . will you really . . . try and . . . understand?" she asked.

The Earl had the feeling that he might be talking to Wendy.

"I promise you that I will try," he said quietly.

* * *

When Olivia went to bed she found it difficult to sleep.

She prayed for a long time that the Earl would *understand* what they had done.

It seemed impossible that the same man, who had behaved as he had, could now understand.

She still winced when she remembered what he had said to her when she called to see him at Chad.

She heard Tony come in.

Getting out of bed, she put on her dressing-gown and went to his room.

"I am sorry to be back so late," Tony said, "but I had a marvellous time and found two horses that Gerry will be mad about when he sees them."

"It will not be a case of whether ... Gerry likes them or not," Olivia said, "but ... whether the Earl does!"

Tony stared at her.

"You mean—he is better?"

"Much better! I had dinner with him, and he is talking about ... seeing what we ... have done either ... to-morrow or the ... next day."

Tony sat down on his bed.

"I knew this would happen," he said, "but I had not expected it quite so soon!"

"Nor did ... I," Olivia admitted, "but I know it is ... all due to ... Mama's herbs."

"He is also very strong," Tony said as if he were working it out in his mind.

"What ... am I to ... say to ... him?" Olivia asked in a frightened voice. "He has been ... so kind to Wendy, but that is not to ... say he will ... be kind to ... Gerry or to me!"

"Do you think he will still insist on your marrying each other?"

"Oh, Tony ... what ... am I to ... do?" Olivia cried. "I love Gerry, but I do ... not wish to *marry* him!"

"The Earl is not going to be pleased that Gerry has paid for my first term at Oxford," Tony said. "That is hardly a necessity where Chad is concerned!"

"No ... of course not!" Olivia agreed. "Nor

134

my . . . gowns from London . . . and all the horses . . . you have . . . bought."

"Now, there I think you are wrong," Tony argued. "Who ever heard of the Earl of Chadwood being without a decent animal to ride or to drive?"

"The present Earl may . . . wish to do things . . . differently from how they . . . were done in . . . the past."

Tony got into bed.

"Well, there is nothing we can do about it," he said. "If he cancels everything, I expect somebody else will try to kill him, and perhaps make a better job of it this time!"

"I am . . . sure that is . . . something you . . . should not say," Olivia expostulated.

"Well, I have said it, and if he turns nasty, you might warn him of the possibility of that happening."

"Of course I could not say . . . anything like . . . that!" Olivia answered. "But . . . I want him to be . . . happy and to . . . enjoy Chad, as we . . . have always . . . done."

As she looked at the expression on her brother's face, she knew that was the truth.

The Earl was brave, as Higgins had told her, and also very handsome.

Why could he not enjoy what the gods had given him just as his ancestors had done?

They had shown mercy and kindness to all those who were dependent on them.

"If only I . . . could make . . . him do . . . that," she whispered.

She was praying that by a miracle that was exactly what would happen.

135

chapter seven

WAITING downstairs, Olivia was very nervous.

Yesterday she had been thankful when the Earl had sent a message to say he was not well enough to get up, as he had hoped.

He said he would let her know the following morning.

She therefore spent the day doing what she thought she should be done before—going to visit the pensioners.

It was a joy beyond words to find how happy they were.

They were thrilled with their repaired cottages and the money they had to spend.

Most of them had some new article of clothing.

They not only looked smarter, but their faces had filled out.

There were not so many lines beneath their eyes as there had been.

Gerry did not appear all day and Tony was, of course, riding.

"If the Earl is getting up," he said, "I am going to ride every minute I have, in case when he sees the horses he either sells them or forbids me to ride them."

Olivia could only agree with him.

But that night, when she went to bed, she prayed that Tony would be allowed to go on riding.

Now she had come downstairs early, wearing one of her new gowns.

She could feel her heart beating in an agitated manner, and her fingers were cold.

There was no sign of Gerry at breakfast.

She thought he, too, was concerned about the Earl.

He would be looking round to make sure that everything was as "ship-shape" as possible.

Even while she was thinking of him she heard the sound of a horse outside the front-door.

A moment later he came into the Sitting-Room.

"Gerry!" she exclaimed. "I missed you at breakfast!"

"I had no time because I was in a hurry," he answered, "and, Olivia, I have something to tell you!"

He shut the door as he spoke, and she looked at him apprehensively.

"What is . . . it?" she asked.

He paused, and she thought, to her surprise, that he was looking very happy.

"I think I ought to start at the beginning," he said, "and tell you that when I went to see Lady Sheldon three days ago, she asked me outright if

I would manage her Estate in the same way as I have done here."

Olivia gasped, then she said:

"Oh, Gerry, what a wonderful idea! Did you accept?"

"Of course I accepted," Gerry replied, "knowing that Lenox is likely to throw me out. Then something else happened!"

"What was that?" Olivia asked.

"I fell in love with Lucinda and she with me!"

Olivia stared at him, thinking she could not have heard him aright.

Then she gave a cry of delight.

"How wonderful! Was it love at first sight, like Papa and Mama?"

"Exactly!" Gerry said. "And I swear to you, Olivia, I would marry her if she had not a penny, because she is the most adorable person I have ever met!"

He smiled before he added:

"But as it is, she is heir to the Sheldon Estate! And the moment we are married, we are taking over everything."

"What does that mean?" Olivia enquired.

"Lady Sheldon is not well, and the Doctors have told her she must go to a warmer climate. Lucinda is her heir, and she has been desperately worried knowing she could not manage alone."

"And now you will manage everything for her!"

"It is going to be very exciting, and almost as big a challenge as it was here."

"It cannot be as bad as that!" Olivia exclaimed.

"Not as regards the welfare of the workers or the pensioners. But the whole Estate needs modernising, which is what I intend to do."

Olivia clasped her hands together.

"Gerry! Gerry! I am so glad for you, and you deserve . . . your happiness."

"You deserve some too," Gerry said, "but we will talk about that later."

He glanced at the clock.

"I am leaving now, as I understand my brother will be coming down soon."

"You are not . . . leaving me to face him . . . alone and without . . . telling him . . . your news?"

"I thought you would like to do that!" Gerry answered.

"You are just being a coward!" Olivia said accusingly.

"Actually I think Lenox will be delighted to be rid of me!" Gerry replied. "And you know I will look after you, but we will discuss this later."

He kissed her cheek and said:

"I am so happy, Olivia, and the whole story is exactly as if it came out of a book!"

"Except that it is true!" Olivia laughed.

She put her arms round his neck and hugged him.

"I am so . . . so happy . . . for you!"

He kissed her again before he said:

"I will come back and see you later to-day, if you have not been torn into small pieces."

Olivia gave a cry.

"Do not . . . frighten me any . . . more than I am . . . already!"

"It will be all right," Gerry said confidently. "If there is a happy ending to my story, there must be one to yours."

"I only . . . hope you are . . . right!" Olivia said in a low voice.

But it was doubtful if Gerry heard, because he was hurrying towards the front-door.

Outside, the groom was holding his horse and he swung himself into the saddle.

Olivia waved to him as he rode away.

She thought no one could look more happy or more pleased with himself.

She sent up a little prayer of gratitude.

Now, where Gerry was concerned, there would be no more problems.

She knew without being told that London would have no more attraction for him.

He would be, as he had said himself, the Boss.

The Sheldon Estate was even bigger than Chad.

If it needed new ideas and modern equipment, it would take a long time to put it in order.

"It is certainly a happy ending for Gerry!" she said beneath her breath.

She walked back into the Sitting-Room.

It was a quarter-of-an-hour later when she was aware that the Earl was coming down the stairs.

The carriage he had ordered was already outside.

Just before he appeared, Bessie had come into the Sitting-Room to say:

"Mrs. Banks be staying at Chad as you and His Lordship are having lunch there."

"Nobody told me," Olivia answered.

"It's what Mr. Higgins said this morning, and her assistant has just arrived to prepare a meal for Miss Wendy and Miss Dawson."

Olivia thought that she herself should have given the orders.

She felt a faint resentment that the Earl was taking over the house.

It was certainly a sign that he was better.

She hastily picked up her bonnet which had been lying on a chair.

She put it on, looking into a mirror on the wall as she did so.

She thought as she looked at her reflection that she looked rather pale.

It was not surprising.

This was the "Day of Reckoning."

If what the Earl said was the "Voice of Doom," neither Gerry nor Tony would be there to hear it.

As the Earl reached the bottom of the stairs, she came from the Sitting-Room towards him.

She saw he was dressed very smartly with the points of his collar high above his chin.

His cravat was tied in an intricate and fashionable style.

He was authoritative and rather overwhelming.

He no longer looked like the man who had been so helpless as he lay unconscious.

As she drew near, she realised she had forgotten how tall he was.

It made her feel not only small, but more nervous than ever.

"Good-morning, Olivia!" the Earl said. "I am looking forward to our drive, and I am glad the sun is shining."

"I only . . . I hope it will . . . not be too . . . much for . . . you," Olivia replied.

"We shall soon find out," the Earl said, "and, needless to say, Higgins is full of gloom!"

Olivia repressed an impulse to suggest in that

case, it might be a good idea to put it off until to-morrow, or for perhaps three or four days.

Then she told herself there was no use funking what her father would have called a "hurdle."

She must just try and jump it, hoping she would not fall on the other side.

The carriage which was waiting outside the front-door was one she knew well.

The old Earl had always used it before he was too ill to leave his bed.

It was large and comfortable.

The two horses drawing it had been at Chad before Gerry and Tony had started to fill the stables with new purchases.

Olivia thought it was tactful of Graves to send horses that would not make the Earl start asking questions.

She stepped into the carriage and the Earl followed her.

The footman put a light rug over their knees.

Olivia expected the Earl would ask her where she wished to take him.

However, the coachman obviously had his orders, and they drove off.

Instead of going towards the village, he drove in through the drive gates.

Just inside in the Park itself was the ancient Church which had been built at the same time as Chad.

Outside the Churchyard stood the Vicarage which looked very different from how it had when the Earl had last seen it.

The roof had been renewed, there was glass in the windows, and the frames had been repainted.

It looked both picturesque and substantial.

The Earl glanced at it as they drove past.

As he asked no questions, Olivia said nothing.

She only looked ahead and thought how lovely the trees were with the deer roaming beneath them.

A little farther on, where the drive curved, they had a perfect view of Chad with the sunshine glittering on the windows.

It was so beautiful and like a Fairy Palace.

Although Olivia was familiar with every brick, the sight of it always seemed to lift her heart.

A flight of white doves flew overhead, then circled down to settle in the garden.

She thought perhaps it was an omen that things would be better than she feared.

Now they could see the lake with the sunshine reflected in it and the swans moving over its silvery surface.

Still the Earl did not speak.

Olivia was afraid to say how lovely it was in case he contradicted her.

"How could he not be thrilled at having the most beautiful home in the world?" she asked herself.

The carriage drew up outside the front-door.

A red carpet had already been run down the steps. There were two footmen waiting to receive them.

Because they had not driven through the village or inspected the Slate Mine, and the Earl had not commented on the Vicarage, Olivia felt very frightened, even more frightened than she had expected to be.

"I am sure he is going to deal with me first!" she told herself.

It was an effort to walk up the steps.

It was even more of an effort to force a smile to her lips as Upton greeted them.

"Good-morning, Miss Olivia!" he said. "And welcome back, M'Lord, to Chad! It's good to see Your Lordship well again!"

"Thank you," the Earl replied.

Upton walked ahead of them and opened the door into the Drawing-Room.

Olivia was expecting to go into the Study.

The Drawing-Room was looking even more attractive than she had anticipated.

There were flowers on almost every table, and the sunshine coming through the open windows glittered on the chandeliers.

Its golden rays were also reflected in the gilt-framed mirrors on the walls.

Olivia walked a little nervously towards the fireplace.

She was acutely aware that the Earl was just behind her.

Then she saw to her surprise that Upton was pouring out two glasses of champagne.

The bottle was standing in a silver wine-cooler on a side-table.

He put the glasses onto a silver salver.

When he offered her one, she took it, aware, as she did so, that her hand was trembling.

The Earl also took a glass, and as Upton had left the room he said:

"I thought, as I have returned safely to Chad, that you might like to repeat the toast you made me the other night when we dined together."

Olivia looked at him in surprise.

This was the first time he had spoken to her since they had left Green Gables.

It was not what she had expected him to say.

He was obviously waiting for an answer, and after a moment she said in a very low voice:

"You . . . know I wish you . . . happiness."

"It is a very big thing to desire," the Earl said.

Olivia drank a little of her champagne, thinking it would give her courage.

"You have . . . so much . . . to make . . . you happy," she said.

"I presume by that you mean material possessions," he answered.

Again it was something which Olivia had not expected him to say.

Because she felt so nervous, she put her glass down on one of the side-tables.

She walked to the window.

Outside the garden in the sunshine was breathtaking.

For a moment she was conscious only that the Earl had followed her and was standing just behind her.

"I am 'Monarch of all I survey!' " he said after a moment. "I am just wondering if that will give me happiness."

"But . . . it must!" Olivia said. "You have so much to do . . . so much to . . . occupy . . . your mind and . . . and your heart."

She stammered over the last words.

She was wondering how she could explain to him how gratifying it would be if he knew his people loved him.

They would serve him not only for the money he

146

paid them, but because they loved him.

"Of course that is what I want!" he said unexpectedly.

She gave a little gasp and looked at him.

"H-how could . . . you know . . . that was . . . what I was . . . thinking?"

"Your thoughts are very obvious to me."

"But . . . you must not . . . read them!" Olivia said quickly without thinking.

"Why not?"

"Because . . . thoughts are . . . private!"

"Your thoughts are not private to me!" the Earl replied. "I found when you were dining with me the other night that I knew what you were thinking, and it was the same the whole way we were driving here."

Olivia put her hands up to her cheeks.

Then, without thinking, as she felt it was in the way, she undid the ribbons of her bonnet.

She threw it down on a chair.

She looked out the window into the garden with unseeing eyes and said:

"If you can . . . read my thoughts . . . then you must know how . . . much I want . . . you to be . . . happy at Chad . . . and to love it as I have loved it . . . ever since I was a child."

The Earl did not speak.

She was afraid that she had said too much and he resented it.

Then he said very quietly:

"There is something I want to ask you, Olivia, and I want you to tell me the truth."

"Of course . . . I will do . . . that," Olivia answered.

"Then turn round and look at me," the Earl said.

She did as he said more because she was surprised than because she wished to obey him.

She looked into his eyes.

There was an expression in them that she did not understand.

"What I want you to tell me," the Earl said, "and you have promised to tell me the truth, is why you did not let me die?"

Because it was so strange a question, Olivia just stared at him.

Then, as she sought for words in which to reply, she knew the answer.

She knew it not with her mind, but with her heart.

It seemed fantastic, incredible! And she was incapable of putting it into words even to herself.

She could only stare at the Earl, and go on staring.

Then slowly, as her heart told her she loved him, the colour spread over her cheeks like the dawn sweeping up the sky.

She loved him!

Of course she loved him!

That was why she had fought to prevent him from dying.

That was why she had so devotedly stopped him from moving and starting his wound bleeding again.

That was why she had watched over him night after night.

That was why she had prayed that he would live.

At first she had hated him, hated him with a

violence she had never known before.

But because he had been helpless, because she had known the Life Force was slipping away from him, she had to hold on to it for him.

She had to make him live even though she was aware that Bessie and Higgins thought there was no hope.

It was love, a love which had surged up within her irresistibly although she had not understood it.

It had turned what seemed to be defeat into a victory as she kept him alive.

The truth flashed through her like fork-lightning.

It was such a revelation that she felt as if the sky itself had opened to tell her the truth.

Then, as her lips could not move and it was impossible to say a word, the Earl said very quietly:

"That is what I hoped was the reason!"

Olivia put her hands onto her breast as if afraid not of him, but of herself.

"I love you!" the Earl said quietly. "So what are we going to do about it?"

Olivia found her voice.

It seemed to come from a very long way away.

"Y-you . . . you love me?" she asked incredulously.

"I love you!" the Earl affirmed. "But like you, I did not know it was love."

"H-how did you . . . know that was . . . what I . . . felt?"

"I have asked myself the same question," he answered. "The answer is quite easy: I knew when I was unconscious that I was in the arms of love. I heard when you talked to me, when you gave me your herbs, that there was love in your voice."

His voice deepened as he went on:

"I did not have to listen to all those people telling me that you had saved my life because I already knew it! I knew it in my heart, and that you saved me, not with medicine but with—love."

Olivia made a little murmur.

She was not certain whether the Earl moved or she did.

But his arms were round her and her face was hidden against his neck.

It was then she knew that she need never be afraid again.

It was so wonderful that she could only tremble against him.

He held her closer and still closer.

Then he said, still in that strange, quiet voice which she found difficult to recognise:

"When you came to me after that insolent swine had tried to kiss you, I knew I had to look after you and protect you."

"That is . . . what I . . . want you . . . to do," Olivia whispered, "but I never . . . thought you would . . . love me."

"I love you," the Earl said firmly, "and I need your love! It is something I have never known, something I have never had, and if you will not give it to me, I shall be sorry I did not die!"

"You are . . . not to . . . say such things!"

Then, as she raised her head, his lips held hers captive.

It was what she had wanted, what she had longed for, but had never put into words.

He kissed her very gently and so lovingly that she felt the tears come into her eyes.

How could she have known, how could she have guessed that the man of her dreams, the man she had thought she would love the moment she saw him, was actually the Earl, who had frightened her.

A man she had believed was menacing her.

A man from whom she had wanted to run away and hide.

The Earl found her lips soft, sweet, and innocent as they surrendered to his.

Holding her closer, his kisses became more demanding and more possessive.

To Olivia it was not only the wonder of his lips and the security of his arms.

His kisses swept away the darkness which had been her fear of the future.

He carried her into a brilliant light that came from Heaven itself.

This was love, the love that was part of the sunshine and the stars, the flowers in the garden, the birds in the sky.

It was everything which had been a part of her since she was born but glittering with an indiscernible rapture.

When the Earl raised his head she said incoherently:

"I love you . . . I love you! Why did I . . . not know I . . . loved you? I have . . . been so . . . afraid you would . . . send us all . . . away!"

"How could I ever have thought of anything so cruel, so wicked?" the Earl asked.

She did not answer, and he pulled her close to him again.

"You have to help me," he said, "you have to teach me, show me how to love as you love."

"I love you because . . . you are you . . . and because you need me," Olivia said, "and if I am never to be afraid again . . . you must not be . . . suspicious that . . . people might . . . hurt you."

The Earl did not answer.

He merely kissed her until they were both breathless.

Then he said:

"How soon can we be married? I want you to myself, without all those other people taking up your thoughts and your time."

Olivia laughed.

"What people?"

"Gerry—for one."

Olivia put up her hand to touch his cheek.

"You need not worry about him," she said. "Gerry is deliriously happy! I was going to tell you, but I was too frightened—he is going to be married!"

"To Lucinda Sheldon?" the Earl asked.

"How do you know that?"

"Higgins said he would not be surprised if that happened, and I was so afraid he might obey my orders and marry you."

"I told you I thought of him as a brother, and Gerry told me just before you came downstairs that he is going to be married immediately."

"And that is what we will do," the Earl said firmly.

There was a silence.

Then Olivia asked:

"You are quite . . . quite certain that you want . . . to marry me? Suppose when you have . . . done so you . . . go back to thinking I am . . . none of your . . . business and wish . . . that you had married . . . somebody else?"

"Do you think that is possible?" the Earl asked. "I have never asked anyone to marry me, and never wanted to marry any other woman. You belong to me. You are mine, and as I can read your thoughts, it will be impossible for youever to find anyone you love better than me without my being aware of it."

"Ishall never love . . . anyone but . . . you!" Olivia promised. "I know that in my mind, my heart, and my soul . . . and I am only upset that I did not . . . realise it . . . when I first . . . saw you."

"You were thinking of your Knight in Shining Armour!" the Earl said as he smiled.

Olivia laughed.

"Did Wendy tell you that?"

"She did, and I was humiliated into believing I was the Ogre and not your Knight."

"I promise that you are . . . my Knight and . . . exactly as I wanted . . . him to . . . be."

"It has tormented me these last days thinking that was what you felt for Gerry."

He, however, did not wait for Olivia to answer.

He kissed her as if he were forcing her to love him more than she did already.

He was wooing her with demanding, passionate kisses!

Once again he was giving her sensations she had never known before.

She felt as if the sunshine were pulsating through her body.

But the ecstasy and glory of it was almost too

much to be borne, and she gave a little murmur and hid her face again.

"My darling, my precious!" the Earl exclaimed. "What have you done to me? I thought I was so self-sufficient and also very controlled. But now I am as helpless in your hands as when I was unconscious!"

"I do . . . I not think that . . . will ever . . . be true," Olivia answered, "and I love you . . . just as you . . . are!"

The Earl kissed her again.

Then he said:

"Now, let us make plans. I expect you can tell me who can marry us immediately. Before you suggest it, I am not waiting until I have appointed a new Vicar in that very smart Vicarage to which you have made so many improvements since I have been ill."

Olivia moved a little closer to him.

"I was so . . . afraid you . . . would be . . . angry . . . about it!"

"I am not angry about anything," the Earl replied.

"Are you . . . quite, quite . . . sure about . . . that?" Olivia asked.

"Quite sure," he answered, "and if you want to tell me what I am not to be angry about, I know it is the Slate Mine, the horses that fill the stables, the doubled pensions for the old people, the repairs to their cottages, and the new methods of farming which have been adopted on all my Farms."

Olivia stared at him in astonishment.

"How . . . can you . . . know all that?" she asked.

The Earl laughed.

"I am intelligent enough to put two and two together! Whether I was unconscious or conscious, everybody who came near me talked! It was Higgins, Bessie, Wendy, Gerry, and I think you can throw in a few birds, bees, and butterflies who all added to what I had learnt already, and the rest I read in your eyes."

Olivia laughed and said:

"It is all too ridiculous! Gerry said everything that was happening was something that either came out of a novelette or a drama in a Playhouse, and he is right!"

She laughed again. Then she said:

"As you know everything I was going to tell you, what are we going to talk about?"

"Getting married!" the Earl answered, and kissed her.

*   *   *

The Earl and Olivia were married three days later by the Vicar of one of the other Parishes on the Estate.

He was a dear old man who had been a close friend of Olivia's Father.

Because the Earl was still, on Higgins's instructions, taking it easy, it was a very secret wedding.

"The whole village will want to celebrate," Olivia had said.

"I know that, my darling," the Earl answered, "but they will have to wait until we return from our honeymoon."

"When will that be?"

"When you are bored with me."

Olivia laughed.

"In that case, the celebrations will have to coincide with our Funerals!"

"There will be plenty of time for feasting and fireworks, and a lot of people making embarrassing speeches," he said.

"We do not want that sort of wedding," Olivia replied, "but the village will want a party."

"They shall have one," the Earl replied, "but not until I feel strong enough and we have been alone together. I want to know my wife a great deal better than I do now."

They had to let Bessie and Higgins into the secret, and, of course, Wendy.

"May I be a bridesmaid? Please, please, 'livia, let me be a bridesmaid!"

"Of course you will," Olivia agreed, "but you are not to breathe a word of what is happening to Miss Dawson, or to her nieces."

Surprisingly it was the Earl who suggested that Miss Dawson and her nieces should all stay at Chad with Wendy while they were away.

"Wendy will love that," Olivia agreed, "and it is such a wonderful house in which to play 'Hide and Seek.' And there are the gnomes and fairies in the garden, and goblins in the wood which one cannot find anywhere else in the whole world."

He kissed her and said:

"You shall introduce them to me as soon as we get back."

"Where are we going?"

"That is a secret!" he replied.

They managed to keep their wedding a secret so cleverly that not even Gerry had the slightest idea what was taking place.

His thoughts were very much occupied elsewhere.

The Earl's carriage took Olivia, Tony, and Wendy from Green Gables to the Church.

Because they might have been seen early in the morning, they were married late in the afternoon.

The men had all come home from work and were having a substantial meal in their cottages.

Olivia wore an exquisite white gown interwoven with silver thread which had come from London.

Her veil was white and had been in the Wood family for generations.

It had been worn by her Mother at her wedding.

There were, she knew, a great number of tiaras in the safe at Chad which had been handed down over the generations.

But Bessie had made her a wreath of white rosebuds from the garden.

Interspersed between them were some of the herbs which had cured so many people in the village.

They were also the herbs which she believed had brought the Earl back to life.

Her bouquet consisted of the same flowers and greenery.

As she walked up the aisle on Tony's arm, the Earl turned to look at her.

There was such an expression of love in his eyes that she felt her heart turning somersaults.

Every nerve in her body responded to him in a way that she could express in only one word, and that was—Love.

Wendy, walking behind her, was also wearing a wreath on her small head.

She looked, the Earl thought, even more like the Angel he had thought her to be when he had first seen her.

When Wendy knew they were to be married, she had flung her arms round the Earl's neck.

"I love 'oo, and if 'oo had waited I would have married 'oo when I was growed up!"

"I think I would have been too old for you," the Earl said as he smiled. "But when you grow up I will give a Ball where you will meet all the most handsome and charming men in England, and choose one to be your Shining Knight."

"I would like that," Wendy said. "And when 'oo's married 'livia I can keep my pony in 'oos stables and, when I'se big, ride 'oos horses."

"Of course you can," the Earl agreed.

Wendy kissed him again, saying:

"I love 'oo, I love 'oo!"

When they were alone, Olivia said:

"I can see in the future . . . I . . . may . . . be jealous of my little sister!"

She was teasing him, but the Earl replied:

"I warn you I shall be very jealous of our sons and daughters if you love them more than me!"

Olivia blushed.

Then she said in a whisper:

"I think because you want . . . love and it is . . . something you never had as a child . . . we must have . . . lots of . . . children who will . . . love you as I do and . . . therefore make . . . you happy."

"I am so happy at the moment," the Earl replied, "that I doubt if I could be any happier, but, of course, I am willing to try!"

He then kissed her until she begged for mercy.

When he released her he said:

"I love, adore, and worship you. Every day I think I am incapable of loving you more, then every hour and every minute I know I was mistaken!"

Now, as the old Priest blessed them, Olivia felt the Earl's fingers tighten on hers.

She was thanking her Father and Mother and God for her happiness.

She was sure that it was entirely due to them that everything had turned out so wonderfully.

Not only would she, Tony, and Wendy be safe in the future, but so would Chad and all the people who belonged to it.

To her surprise, when they came out of the Church, there was not one carriage, but two standing outside.

Before she and the Earl got into the first one, Tony and Wendy kissed her good-bye.

"It was a lovely wedding," Tony said, "and I know you will both be very happy!"

He shook the Earl's hand as he spoke.

Wendy flung her arms round his neck and kissed him a dozen times.

"I'se been a bridesmaid," she said triumphantly, "and I love 'oo!"

"You must look after Chad until Olivia and I come back," the Earl told her. "Tony will see to the horses and you are to see to everything in the house."

"I'll do that," Wendy promised proudly.

The Earl helped Olivia into the carriage, and as they drove off she asked:

"What is happening? Where are we going?"

"We are spending our first night," he said, "in

a very special place, where I first loved you, and thought you loved me too."

Olivia looked at him in astonishment.

"Do you . . . mean . . . Green Gables?"

"Of course!" he said. "It is a house of love, and that is where I want to start my honeymoon, before we carry our love to the other houses I own."

"Oh, darling, only you could think of anything so wonderful!" Olivia said.

"We will be alone," the Earl said. "If we had stayed at Chad, there would have been the congratulations of the staff, but for the moment I want to think only of you, and for you to think only of me!"

"We can do . . . that at . . . Green Gables," Olivia said.

She was to find when they got there that there were only Bessie and Higgins to look after them.

They had already said all there was possible to say about their marriage.

Therefore, as the Earl had intended, Olivia had only to think of him.

They ate a delicious dinner which, of course, had been provided by Mrs. Banks from Chad.

They sat in the small Dining-Room, talking by the light of the candles, as they had when they had dined together upstairs.

When dinner was over, without even discussing it they went upstairs.

They would start their married life in the bedroom where the Earl had lain unconscious and where Olivia had held him in her arms.

When she entered the room she gave a gasp because, although it was so familiar, the Earl had filled it with dozens and dozens of Madonna Lilies.

Their fragrance scented the air.

There were great vases of them on each side of the bed, and a huge arrangement on the table and on the chest of drawers.

"Oh, Darling, it is so romantic!" Olivia exclaimed.

"What can be more appropriate for you than the flower which stands for purity and love?" the Earl asked.

He kissed her, then went to the Dressing-Room.

It was where Higgins had slept when he was so ill, and where her Father had once dressed.

Olivia put on a pretty nightgown and loosened her hair so that it fell over her shoulders.

Then she pulled back the curtains and slipped into bed.

All the candles had been lit, but because she was shy, she left only one burning by the bed.

It reminded her of the night she had entered the room to find Wendy asleep in the Earl's arms.

It was where she wanted to be herself.

He came in, looking so large and handsome with such a look of happiness on his face that it transformed his whole appearance.

He did not resemble in the least the man of whom she had once been afraid and thought she hated.

He stood looking at her.

"I thought when I first saw Wendy," he said, "that she was an Angel, but now I know she was only a Cherub and at last I have the Angel for whom I was looking."

"She is . . . waiting for you . . . darling," Olivia said, and held out her arms.

He got in beside her and drew her close to him.

She thought because he was touching her that he carried her up to the stars shining overhead.

From this day on their lives would be transformed.

Everything that was ordinary and usual would become an enchanted Heaven.

It was of such beauty and wonder, it would be difficult to believe they were still alive.

"I . . . love . . . you!" she whispered against the Earl's lips.

As he held her so close to him that she could hardly breathe, he said as if he had been reading her thoughts:

"You are not real—you are Love itself, and it is a love so perfect, so glorious, we are no longer human."

Then he was kissing her eyes, her cheeks, her neck, and her breasts.

"Love me . . . Oh, my wonderful . . . husband . . . love me!" Olivia cried.

As the Earl made her his, she knew that her wish had come true.

He had found happiness, a happiness he had never known before.

It was a happiness which came from God, was part of God, and was in fact—LOVE.

ABOUT THE AUTHOR

Barbara Cartland, the world's most famous romantic novelist, who is also an historian, playwright, lecturer, political speaker and television personality, has now written over 558 books and sold over 600 million copies all over the world.

She has also had many historical works published and has written four autobiographies as well as the biographies of her mother and that of her brother, Ronald Cartland, who was the first Member of Parliament to be killed in the last war. This book has a preface by Sir Winston Churchill and has just been republished with an introduction by Sir Arthur Bryant.

Love at the Helm, a novel written with the help and inspiration of the late Earl Mountbatten of Burma, Great Uncle of His Royal Highness The Prince of Wales, is being sold for the Mountbatten Memorial Trust.

She has broken the world record for the last sixteen years by writing an average of twenty-three books a year. In the *Guinness Book of Records* she is listed as the world's top-selling author.

Miss Cartland in 1978 sang an Album of Love Songs with the Royal Philharmonic Orchestra.

In private life Barbara Cartland, who is a Dame of the Order of St. John of Jerusalem, Chairman of the St. John Council in Hertfordshire and Deputy President of the St. John Ambulance Brigade, has fought for better conditions and salaries for Midwives and Nurses.

She championed the cause for the Elderly in 1956 invoking a Government Enquiry into the "Housing Conditions of Old People."

In 1962 she had the Law of England changed so that Local Authorities had to provide camps for their own Gypsies. This has meant that since then thousands and thousands of Gypsy children have been able to go to School, which they had never been able to do in the past, as their caravans were moved every twenty-four hours by the Police.

There are now fourteen camps in Hertfordshire and Barbara Cartland has her own Romany Gypsy Camp called Barbaraville by the Gypsies.

Her designs "Decorating with Love" are being sold all over the U.S.A. and the National Home Fashions League made her, in 1981, "Woman of Achievement."

She is unique in that she was one and two in the Dalton list of Best Sellers, and one week had four books in the top twenty.

Barbara Cartland's book *Getting Older, Growing Younger* has been published in Great Britain and the U.S.A. and her fifth cookery book, *The Romance of Food,* is now being used by the House of Commons.

In 1984 she received at Kennedy Airport America's Bishop Wright Air Industry Award for her contribution to the development of aviation. In 1931 she and two R.A.F. Officers thought of, and carried, the first aeroplane-towed glider airmail.

During the war she was Chief Lady Welfare Officer in Bedfordshire looking after 20,000 Service men and women. She thought of having a pool of Wedding Dresses at the War Office so a Service Bride could hire a gown for the day.

She bought 1,000 gowns without coupons for the A.T.S., the W.A.A.F.'s and the W.R.E.N.S. In 1945 Barbara Cartland received the Certificate of Merit from Eastern Command.

In 1964 Barbara Cartland founded the National Association for Health of which she is the President, as a front for all the Health Stores and for any product made as alternative medicine.

This is now a £65 million turnover a year, with one-third going in export.

In January 1988 she received *La Médaille de Vermeil de la Ville de Paris.* This is the highest award to be given in France by the City of Paris. She has sold 25 million books in France.

In March 1988 Barbara Cartland was asked by the Indian Government to open their Health Resort outside Delhi. This is almost the largest Health Resort in the world.

Barbara Cartland was received with great enthusiasm by her fans, who fêted her at a reception in the City, and she received the gift of an embossed plate from the Government.

Barbara Cartland was made a Dame of the Order of the British Empire in the 1991 New Year's Honours List by Her Majesty, The Queen, for her contribution to Literature and also for her years of work for the community.